BUCKFOOLZ

BUCKFOOLZ

Homer McMillian

Copyright © 2017 by Homer McMillian

All rights reserved. No part of this book may be reproduced or transmitted in any form or by any means, electronic or mechanical, including photocopying, recording, or by any information storage and retrieval system without the written permission of the author, except where permitted by law.

This is a work of fiction. The characters, incidents and dialogue are drawn from the author's imagination and are not to be construed as real. Any resemblance to actual events or persons, living or dead, is entirely coincidental.

ISBN: 13-978-1979571081

Cover Designer: Rochelle Sodipo Washington
Editor: Je Tuan Jones

DEDICATION

This book is dedicated to my beloved sister Victoria Mack a.k.a. WOPPIE. Her dream to become a published author lives through me. Until we meet again...

ACKNOWLEDGMENTS

I would like to thank the Almighty Creator. In my darkest hours he offered me light. Thank to my parents Homer and Bernice McMillian for their love and understanding, I'm forever grateful.

To my wife Beatriz for being there for me and bringing me back to earth when I needed it. To my daughters –Tina, Alleayah, Victoria, and Elizabeth – and my sons – Brandon and Justin – and my grandson Jason Williams, I love you.

Thank you to my family and friends: my sister Vernice, my nephew ray McMillian, my niece Kimberly, Rodriquez and her kids – Brianna, Brittney, and Brian – also thank you to Lyndella Parrot, James Mack (Brother In-law), and Yolanda Florence, I will forever be thankful for your support.

Last but not least, a very special thanks to Mrs. Je Tuan Jones for guidance and Mrs. Rochelle Sodipo Washington for the dope book cover.

TABLE OF CONTENTS

Chapter 1 1

Chapter 2 3

Chapter 3 13

Chapter 4 21

Chapter 5 35

Chapter 6 43

Chapter 7 51

Chapter 8 61

Chapter 9 67

Chapter 10 77

Chapter 11 83

Chapter 12 97

Chapter 13 101

Chapter 14 105

Chapter 15 111

Chapter 16 121

Chapter 17 125

Chapter 18 129

Chapter 19 135

Chapter 20 141

Chapter 21 145

Chapter 22 151

Chapter 23 159

Epilogue..167

About the Author 171

Contact the Author...173

CHAPTER 1

It is said that the road to freedom can be long and treacherous, winding through bumpy hills and valleys... if you asked Buck, though, he would have told whoever came up with that load of crap to shut the hell up. The road to freedom felt damned good, and nobody could tell him otherwise. The window to his cherry red truck was down as the latest Southern trap music boomed through his speakers. It also wasn't some long and treacherous road. He'd seen enough of those from Lumpkin, Georgia. Oh, hell no, these roads were wondrous and beautiful.

He was driving into New York: it didn't get any better than this. This shit looked just like what he'd seen on TV and the internet. There were people every damned where, and no one cared about you. Back home, when you passed a car, you looked inside the car to see if you knew them. Here, in New York, people kept their eyes on the road. If they looked at you, it was to see what kind of idiot would drive so slowly. Buck could get used to this.

Who was going to talk about him now? Everyone back

HOMER MCMILLIAN

home saw him as a momma's boy who didn't want to work. Things were different. Now, he was a real estate owner who'd already seen more of the world on his road trip to New York than 95% of his hometown's population. Things were about to change. His life was headed in a new direction. Everyone who ever doubted him could kiss his ass.

CHAPTER 2

Sometimes opportunity just falls into your lap... other times, all of your dreams for a better future come crumbling down.

"Hell, nah."

Buck shook his head and tried not to scream as he looked out on his new land. Instead, he threw his black fitted cap on to the concrete and rubbed his hands down his face. *Why would my Uncle leave me some bullshit like this?* Buck continually shook his head in disbelief and tried to calm his nerves.

"Dude, get the fuck out the middle of the street. You look like an idiot," someone down the road shouted at him.

Buck closed his eyes and tried to keep his cool. He'd heard a lot about New York dudes, and he didn't want to get into any fights. His anger was already high; he wasn't in the mood to be tested by anybody. Buck spat on his property, turning to whoever made the rude remark.

"I ain't in the middle of the street, I'm on the sidewalk."

His eyes scanned a tall man, surely over six feet tall,

dressed in a white T-shirt, jeans, and some awfully expensive gym shoes. Buck almost came on himself when he took a closer look: they were special edition Jordans: the fourth edition, black and red. He'd wanted those for the longest time, but wasn't willing to stand in line or pay a car note to get them.

"You lookin' at my shoes like you want em' or something," the man said as he stuck his chest out and palmed his fist.

Buck tried to keep from laughing. The boy's false bravado only showed his age. The boy couldn't have been any older than 18. He wasn't a man... he was just some kid trying to seem older. Buck didn't take his eyes off him, though, because he'd watched The Wire. It didn't matter how old kids were, they could still get you. Buck wasn't about that fighting life. Sure, he'd gotten into a few fist fights in his life, but nothing much more. Instead of shooting a rude remark back, he chose to play it safe.

"My bad." Buck's southern accent came out heavy and slow, like molasses. "I'm just looking at the land right here."

"Why? You thinking about buying it or something? It ain't worth shit," the boy shrugged. "Shit is crazy expensive around here, so I don't think you would want it anyway. If you're going to spend money, then spend it on something you can actually do something with."

"It's too late for that."

Buck wished he could have had the money instead. The boy was right.

"Where in the hell are you from? You from Mississippi, or something? You sound like one of them country dudes."

Buck gave an easy grin that showed off his pearly white teeth (with the exception of the gold one on the bottom row).

"Naw, I'm from Georgia. This land is mine now. My uncle died and left it to me."

"Well I feel sorry for you because it ain't shit you can do with it unless he left you mad money, too. Good luck, homie," the boy said and walked on, shaking his head as if he pitied Buck.

How could Buck argue with that? He would have loved it if the boy were wrong, but the knot in his stomach only tightened more. He was standing in Brooklyn, in front of a shitty piece of land that was right in the middle of two project buildings. He assumed they were project buildings, anyway. They didn't have any buildings like that were he was from.

At least he knew he was in the middle of the hood. People walked by him, engrossed in their own lives, completely oblivious to the hopelessness he felt. Instead of standing on the sidewalk or making any more of a scene, he returned to his trailer with a heavy sigh. He drove 18 hours to see nothing. How was he supposed to call his mama and let her know she wasted her money? She had spent a huge chunk on a trailer for him to drive to New York, all so he could have a better life. He had told her that their luck was about to change, that he would send her some money back or send for her when he struck it rich.

The only thing that he'd gotten was another problem. He didn't know the first thing about building on property, especially one like this. Now that he thought about it, he had no game plan at all. *What was I expecting in the first place? I don't know how real estate here works. I don't even know how to sell this shit.* For the first time in a long time, Buck didn't see a way to weasel his way out of things. He was far from home, and didn't have anybody or any answers. Why would his uncle leave him a piece a land that he couldn't do anything with?

Buck walked to the small bathroom on the brand-new trailer and looked at himself in the mirror. The bathroom barely had enough room for him to move around. It consisted of a small sink with a cabinet beneath it. The toilet was so close that they were practically kissing one another. The tub was on the opposite side, accompanied by a clean brown-white shower curtain. Buck sighed and leaned over the sink. *Damn, what am I going to do?* His locks fell to his shoulders in perfect uniformity. They were his pride and joy. When he started growing them, people judged him for it. They still judged him, but he didn't care.

It was his hair, and he always kept it looking neat.

He splashed water on his coffee-colored face and shook his head. *I've really done it, now.* Reality came crashing down on him like a ton of bricks. He had made false promises to his mama and had no idea what to do. Just like everything else, he walked into a situation with his eyes closed.

Buck opened the cabinet and brushed his teeth. He should have done it earlier, but the excitement of finally getting to his destination was too much to bear. Now, he realized that he not only could have brushed his teeth, but he could have showered, too. He laughed with a mouth full of foam as he thought about the property that awaited outside. Only his life would consist of such ridiculousness. Why did he think that his life was about to drastically change for the better? He was going to have to work smart for he wanted. There was no way in hell that he was going back home with his tail between his legs. He was in the land of hustlers, and he was going to make it happen.

He was 28 years old and had practically nothing to show for it. His mom's nickname for him was Peter Pan. According to her, he never wanted to grow up. Why should he have to? Life was good, and he wanted to enjoy it. How could he enjoy his life working all the time? His mom would never admit it, but she didn't seem to mind taking care of him. He was the baby of the family and her only son, so she spoiled him.

He loved being spoiled, but even he knew that it was time to stop leeching off his mother. Buck promised himself that after she had purchased him the brand-new RV, it was going to be the last huge thing she'd buy him. Well, after she gave him money for gas... and some spending money. Hey, a man had to eat and make sure he got to New York safely. His mom was a nurse, so she wasn't hurting financially, but she wasn't rich, either.

"Think," he urged at his reflection after he gargled mouthwash. The unfamiliar feeling of anxiety crept into his stomach, and he didn't like it. He needed to figure something out as soon as humanly possible.

He wiped his face and headed into the trailer. It was beautiful; his mother went all out for him. There was a room in the front with a king size bed and entertainment center. It had a U-shaped dinette across from the kitchen area and bathroom. Next to the dinette was a brown leather couch. In the very back was a room with another entertainment center and two leather couches. Those two couches folded out into beds.

New York was filled with people that needed places to sleep, right? Maybe he could sell room on his RV. It was a crazy idea, but shit, he'd seen far crazier. His trailer was probably bigger and nicer than at least half of the residences in New York. His place was better than the buildings that he was currently parked in front of, right? With that in mind, he got out of his RV and headed to his big, shiny red pickup truck that pulled it.

When he opened the door, there were two men standing outside, sizing the trailer up.

"Hello," Buck said with an easy grin.

"This big motherfucker yours?" the shorter of the two men asked. The man couldn't have been any taller than 5'5; Buck felt like his own 5'10 frame towered over his. He always felt sorry for short men. It seemed like life gave them the short end of the stick, in every sense of the word. He wasn't tall by any stretch of the imagination, but he was tall enough for most women, and that's all that mattered.

"Yeah, it's mine," Buck said, "I'm Buck. It's nice to meet the both of ya."

The two men looked at one another as if they were confused. Obviously, they were confused by his friendly manner.

"Well, Buck," the taller guy said, "It's nice to meet you, too. I'm Ron. We came to tell you that your big-ass truck is blocking way too many spots. When do you plan on moving this thing?"

Buck put his hands up as if he were surrendering: "I'm getting ready to move it right now. So sorry for the inconvenience. You two have a beautiful day." The short one laughed.

"Where are you from?"

"I'm from Lumpkin. Georgia."

"That's a real place?" Ron asked. "That's some real hillbilly shit."

"I guess you could say I'm a hillbilly, but you'd be surprised at how technology has helped us advance... we use internet and everything. I just saw a cell phone for the first time about a year ago, and it just really blew my mind. Now, they're telling me people have watches that work as phones. Have you ever seen one??"

"Dude, really?" Ron looked at him with a screwed-up face.

Buck laughed. "You two have a great day! I've gotta move my big-ass... truck out of the way."

Before the other two could say another word, Buck hopped into his truck and drove off, dragging the RV behind him.

His hands gripped the steering tightly. Why did everyone assume anyone from the south was ignorant? He could probably think circles around them. He didn't like to work hard, but he was no dummy. His mom had put him in private schools long before she could ever really afford them. He wasn't in the top of his classes academically, but that was only because he didn't see the point in working hard when he could coast through classes and still pass. Who cared about the grade, as long as you got your diploma? The same ideology got him his Associates degree, too. Hard work was for the people who didn't know how to relax. He didn't have that problem and didn't need to prove anything to anyone.

For now, he needed to focus on rustling up on some roommates. At least he could make an income that way.

CHAPTER 3

Buck drove around aimlessly; as if he could afford the gas money. After about a half hour, he realized that he had no idea where he was going. Paying for a hotel was crazy when he had a huge RV attached to his truck. Space was limited in New York, and there weren't many places he could park without getting a ticket.

"I'm stupid as hell," he thought, laughing out loud. Buck didn't have to find anywhere to put his trailer, he had a piece of land that he could place his truck on. He turned around and headed back to his small piece of property. It wasn't much, and it wasn't big, but it was enough. He eventually got to the block and pulled his truck onto the rocky land.

"Home, sweet home." A triumphant smile flashed across his face as he climbed from the truck and headed to the RV. The comfortable leather seats practically begged for his attention, and he really wanted to play his X-box. Still, there were things he needed to be done. He couldn't slack off anymore. Instead, he showered, changed clothes, and grabbed what he needed. It was time to do some sightseeing and greeting people in the neighborhood.

People walked by and stared as if he'd sprouted another head. *They can look at me all they want, this is my shit. If I want to park on it on put a tent on it, I can do that. I don't get what the big deal is anyway, haven't these people seen a trailer before? Maybe I'm not the only one that needs to get out more.* Buck smiled to himself and headed down the street. He was ready to explore more of what Brooklyn had to offer.

"So, you're just going to leave your trailer right there?" He heard a voice say.

What was up with everyone questioning him? He was used to people being in his business back home, but it wasn't what he expected in New York. Weren't people supposed to mind their own business and not care about what you do? He turned around to see who was talking, and was greeted by three women.

"Sooo, you gonna answer the question or nah?" The redbone in the middle said.

He couldn't help but grin goofily at them. All three were pretty, but the one to the left was jaw-droppingly gorgeous.

"Yeah, I'm leaving it right there. I can do that."

The chocolate-skinned beauty to the left smacked her lips. She was the kind of beautiful you saw only in a black movie. Her skin practically glowed. Her box braids were pulled into a high ponytail that fell to the middle of her back. She looked at him with a mixture of annoyance and humor on her face.

"You can't do that. You can't just park your big-ass shit on that lot and leave it there."

This was too easy. Already, he knew it was an excellent decision. "It's my property." Buck kept his face straight.

"Oh, really? You're trying to tell me that you own that property? I've lived here all my life and I ain't never seen you. Where in the hell you been?" The chocolate beauty raised a perfectly-arched eyebrow.

Buck shifted from one foot to the other nervously. Chicks usually didn't make him nervous, but she was turning up the temperature. She was sexy even when she was being rude. The women back home weren't like her - they weren't so damned feisty. Also, being feisty with a man they barely knew was out of the question. The women back home were nice and saved their attitudes for their kids and husbands. Oddly enough, he kinda liked the attitude.

"My uncle Larry died and left it to me. So, here I am. I came to check it out, see how it was, and now I think I'm gonna stay a while," Buck answered honestly.

"I heard you're from Bumpkin, Georgia... is that true?" she asked.

"No... I mean yeah, but no," he said.

"Which is it? Yes or no?" she asked impatiently.

Buck stared at her dreamily. He wondered how old she was. She didn't look like she could have been older than twenty-five. She certainly looked grown, probably in her early to mid-twenties. Her blue cotton crop-top tee and high-waisted jeans showed off all her curves. They were enough to spark his imagination, for sure. He could imagine having her in his King bed already.

"Hello?" she said, interrupting his thoughts. "You gonna answer or not?"

"Oh! I'm from Lumpkin, Georgia, not Bumpkin." She waved dismissively and laughed.

"Same damned thing. So how long do you plan on staying?"

"Why? You plan on seeing me more, or something?" he asked. His question got an immediate response from her friends. They snickered and made the kind of remarks silly women make when they aren't the one getting a man's attention.

"That's a negative. I just wanted to know how long this big-ass trailer was gonna be here," she responded. "The kids around here play there."

Okay, now she was starting to hurt him a little. He just met the damned girl, so why should he give a rat's ass what she thought? He quickly changed his tone as he realized he was being played in front of people.

"Well, it's gonna sit there until I'm ready to move it," he said sternly. "Why are you so worried about it anyway? You live there? You in need of shelter?"

The snickers that her friends gave turned into rambunctious laughter.

Silly chicks. If there was one thing that Buck couldn't stand, it was a silly chick. It was one thing to have a sense of humor... it was another to act like you were 5.

"Oh, well excuse me," she said as she took a dramatic step back. "Didn't mean to get you all in your feelings. I'm Shante."

"Nice to meet you, Shante. I'm Buck."

Her friends howled with laughter again, and she gave them a look like they were being rude.

"These two fools are Lexi and Nikki. I'm sorry; sometimes they gotta act like they don't have any manners."

Buck looked at her two physically inferior friends and gave a slight nodded, "Hi."

"Sorry, I didn't mean to be rude. It's just that I didn't expect your name to be Buck. Like, really. You're from the country, you have a trailer, and your name is Buck," Lexi giggled though her gapped teeth. All the appeal that Lexi had went out the window - not because of the gap, either.

"I'm sorry, excuse me if I don't get the joke," Buck said as he shrugged. Before the other woman could say anything, he made his exit. "It's nice to meet all of you, but I'm about head on my way. Enjoy your day."

"Yeah, you too, Buck." Shante emphasized the end of his name. "See you around."

Buck walked away without giving it a second thought. The thrill was gone. He didn't have time for chicks who laughed at him. Just like that, he missed the women back home, although he hadn't treated them very well, either. Most of them claimed that he was too distant and wasn't serious enough. He just liked to laugh and have a good time. It wasn't his fault if they were too uptight. Life was meant to be enjoyed, and sometimes a man just wanted to play his game all day, not listen to some bickering, whining woman. The sooner women understood that, the better off they would be.

His mother often told him he was confused because he didn't like women that were too silly... or too serious. He was destined to be alone and screw random chicks from different counties that he met in shady lounges. That life did him just fine because he didn't have to answer to anyone. He could keep his place exactly the way he liked it. He didn't have to worry about sharing his bathroom or anything. Whenever 10 a.m. rolled around, it was always time to send the woman out or take her home... after she cooked breakfast, of course. A man had to eat! It was the least she could do, after all; she got a free night's stay at his place and the ride of a lifetime.

He headed down the street, feeling like a boss. He wasn't about to let some woman that he barely knew trip him up. What was up with women thinking they could do that, anyway? With one smile, they'd try to wrap you around their finger. Still, she seemed interested at the very moment that he lost interest. He was going to see her again, but if she wanted him at all, she was going to have to do the chasing. He was over it. That shit was way overrated. Why let women think that they ran things? That was a negative.

CHAPTER 4

For the next hour, Buck roamed around Brooklyn. His eyes couldn't take enough in. All of it was too good to be true. There were so many people walking around, totally oblivious to one another. One thing that he did notice, though, was that people were a lot nicer here than they were in movies. Everyone claimed that people in New York were cut throat, but whenever he asked someone something, they took the time to inform him.

It was a pleasant surprise. I mean, some people gave him a look as if he was a dumb tourist. Shit, it was confusing. You could walk down a block and get lost; well, he could. There was just so much to see! The further he walked, the whiter Brooklyn got, and the more expensive it felt. He was no stranger to that. Gentrification was a bitch. White people buy up the property, claiming they're going to make it better, then they push all of the black people out and raise the prices. It looked beautiful, but he couldn't imagine the locals being too excited about it. Not being able to afford the services in your own neighborhood wasn't cool. Then having people consistently raise your rent was enough to make you lose it!

He stopped inside a Deli because his stomach wasn't playing any games. It was prissy as hell. Why did people need to be in the lap of luxury to order a damned sandwich? Order the fucking sandwich and go on about your business. When he looked at the prices on the chalkboard, he almost coughed up a lung. *These fuckers are some real hustlers!* Shit, with these prices there better be two bitches in the back giving happy endings. Why would one sandwich, one damned sandwich, cost thirteen dollars? He could get an entire loaf of bread and a pound of honey-baked ham for half that!

Buck held on to the debit card, second-guessing whether he wanted a corned beef on rye at all. Even if it was just this one time, he had to know what a thirteen-dollar sandwich tasted like. When he got to the counter, the blonde perky girl behind it wore a lime green shirt that matched the white and lime green decor. He was smart enough to know excellent branding when he saw it. That was what he studied in college.

"Hello! Welcome to The Fresh Palace! How can I help you? Would you like to sample our new Mango Pineapple smoothie? It's so delicious because it has real mango and pineapples in it. Also, it's milk-based, so it's super creamy!" The girl smiled liked there really were two bitches in the back giving happy endings.

What in the hell was she talking about? Milk-based? He was going to turn her down, but it sounded good as hell, and sample meant free.

"Yeah, I'll sample that."

"Awesome!" she smiled as she grabbed a tiny sample cup and handed it to him. "I just made this batch five minutes ago, so it should still taste excellent... and it's fresh, just like everything else here."

He lifted the cup to his lips. It reminded him of the sample cups inside of Sam's Club. Man, he loved it in there. You could walk in there hungry on a Saturday morning and leave full. It wasn't that he didn't have food at home! It was just free, and he could shop for random stuff. It was the highlight of his Saturday mornings. After that, he made a trip to Walmart and get his day going.

"That's really good," he said as his taste buds lit up.

"I thought you would like it. Would you consider purchasing one along with your order today?" she asked.

"Yeah, give me the biggest one you've got. I'll also take a corned beef on rye," he said confidently. He dug into his pocket and pulled out his wallet.

"Excellent choice! That will be $19.74."

Buck paused. Everything within him was telling him to put his wallet back in his pocket and walk out of the store. Yeah, he had it, but he was about to spend twenty dollars on one sandwich and drink. He'd clearly lost his mind. It didn't matter; it was too late. He was at the counter and wasn't going to embarrass himself by being a cheapskate. He handed over the card, took his card back, and returned it to his brown leather wallet.

"Thanks so much for your business. Just walk down to the end of the counter. Your order will be delivered there."

He nodded and went where she directed him. He could see them in the back preparing his order, but still couldn't shake the feeling that he was being taken for a ride. *Twenty fuckin' dollars. This is crazy.*

Next to him stood a white man in a blue suit who looked frazzled. He was talking on the phone. Buck tried not to eavesdrop, but it was hard because the man sounded pissed. His clothes were nice; he seemed pretty well off. It was clear that he spent a grip on the suit he was wearing, but he had a hardened face. Not in the sense of looks, really. Buck knew what stress looked like, and the dude had it written all over him.

The man in the suit sighed into the phone, "Okay, thank you for your time. I appreciate the opportunity to interview with you. No... I understand. Things are tight right now, and the competition was stiff. In the future, if there are any positions open, I ask that you keep my resume on file. Of course, yes. You have a great day, as well." He ended the call and, with some restraint, cursed loudly.

"FUCK!"

All eyes shifted to the man in the suit, but it was clear he didn't give a shit. He banged his hand on the counter and kept on.

"Can I ever get a fuckin' break?" He ran his hand through his hair frantically. Buck felt sorry for the man.

"Are you gonna be okay?"

"No. No, I'm not going to be okay. This is the fourth call that I've gotten this week turning me down for a position. The fourth! Most of them don't even call, so you can just imagine how many interviews I've been on. This is absolute bullshit. I swear to God, I'm thinking about jumping from the roof of the building I'm about to get evicted from. I may as well go out in style. Fuck this... fuck all of it." His voice trembled, and his eyes were wide. He hit the counter again, this time with enough force to shake the napkin holder, pacing in a tight circle.

Buck's eyes widened. "Don't do anything crazy. Things will get better. I'm sorry that you're having such a shitty day. I mean, mine isn't going too well, either. I'm here from Georgia, was supposed to be here getting some property from my uncle, but man… the property is a piece of shit. I drove all the way here on a blank mission. I ain't got no job, and I can't go back home. I know all about stress, but I'm not about to jump off a building. Now you're just acting out." The man shook his head and slumped his shoulders in defeat.

"I just don't know what to do anymore."

"How about we sit down, eat this overpriced food, and talk about it," Buck suggested.

The man was sizing him up. Buck was alright with that. He was used to dealing with white people, even racist white people.

"I know I don't look like one of your buddies, but I'm cool," Buck laughed.

"How do you know what my friends look like?" the man asked.

"I don't, I'm just assuming they're as white as you."

The man laughed, "I have a Mexican friend, too."

"That shit don't count, especially if you can only count one. See, you need to talk to me, that way you can have two minority friends."

"Sounds like a plan. I'm Stan, by the way." Stan held his hand out.

"I'm Buck." He extended his hand and returned his firm handshake.

The barrier between the two strangers came crashing down. Stan was the first guy Buck liked in New York. He wasn't judgmental and hadn't asked him about his accent.

"Mango Pineapple smoothie and a tuna salad," a man said from behind the counter.

"Damn," Buck laughed, "they got you with that damned smoothie too, huh?"

"I did my best to resist, but I couldn't say no to the free sample. Right now, I need all the freebies I can get, not spend money on shit like this. They get me like this every time I come here."

"This sandwich better make me want to slap my momma, for as much as I paid," Buck said.

"This stuff here will make you want to fight your mom in the street. You won't be disappointed."

"I hope you're right. I almost walked my ass up out of here." Buck's stomach grumbled in protest.

"Mango Pineapple smoothie and a corned beef on rye," the man announced from behind the counter.

"That's me," Buck grabbed his tray.

He and Stan headed for a table towards the back of the restaurant. They spread out their food, looked at one another tentatively, and bit in. Buck practically moaned when the fresh corned beef, delicious mustard, and perfect bread practically melted in his mouth.

"Damn," he said while the food was still in his mouth. His eyes rolled into the back of his head. "This shit is good."

Stan laughed. "Told ya." They ate in silence for a couple of minutes before Buck started the conversation again.

"So, what's the deal with you, man? Why are you thinking about jumping off of a building?"

Stan sighed, "I'm not really gonna jump... I just was angry."

"All of that stuff starts out with a thought. One minute you're making jokes about it, and then the next minute you're standing on top of that building, and it's not so funny anymore," Buck told him.

But had first-hand experience in this area. His father shot himself in the head when the guy was only twelve years old. His dad had a lot of issues, and drinking was one of the main problems. There were so many nights where his dad would jokingly say that he wished he could just end it all. None of them took him seriously because he usually had a smirk on his face and was in a drunken stupor. He, his mom, and older sisters would just send him to bed.

Buck couldn't focus on his father because he was too busy trying to cheer his mom and sisters up. Having a ranting, raving alcoholic in the house brought the vibe down, so he did everything he could to keep them laughing. His mom often said that he was her joy. Being the "joy" of the family got him into a ton of trouble at school because teachers didn't appreciate it so much.

"I'm guessing that you lost someone?" Stan asked, studying his face.

"Yeah, my dad, sixteen years ago. That's why I don't play around when people say stuff like that. You live by yourself?"

Stan nodded, "Yeah. I was married till my wife left me a few years ago. She said that I worked too much. If I knew that I was going to get laid off, then I would have spent more time with her. Now, I don't have a damned thing. I'm about to live on the street if something doesn't come through soon."

"Damn, that's messed up. Life can really kick you in the balls when you're down. You ain't got no family you can stay with?"

"I would rather live in a cardboard box than stay with my family. Bunch of crazy drug addicts." Stan took a sip from his smoothie. "I don't talk to them much. I like to keep it that way. The would only beg me for money that I don't have. They're part of the reason I'm in this mess. I spent most of my money fixing their messes, and now that I'm in need of help, I don't have anyone."

"So... how about you move with me?" Buck said quickly. Stan looked at him in confusion.

"What?"

"Move in with me. I have a trailer on my property, so the cost won't be crazy."

Stan stared at him incredulously and shook his head. "Thanks, but no thanks."

"Why not? You said it yourself: you don't have anywhere to go. The planets have aligned, you've got a place. Why spit in the face of God?" Buck couldn't help but lay it on thick. Stan laughed.

"Spit in the face of God? You sell cars, or something?

You really made me feel bad with that line. You're good."

"I'm not trying to pull one over on you. I just think this is a good look for the both of us. You need a place to stay, I need tenants." Buck tried to keep the desperation out of his voice. He needed friends, as well. He hadn't been in New York for a full 24 hours yet and already felt lonely. They ate in silence for a few moments.

"I can't believe I'm thinking about moving into a trailer with someone that I just met. "I've truly hit rock bottom."

"Damn, tell me how you really feel. You don't have to do it, but I figured that, at three fifty a month, it's a steal." Buck threw his hands up. Begging wasn't something he would do. If Stan wanted to let the opportunity pass him by, that was on him.

"Three fifty?"

"Yeah, but I have to be honest, it's just a pull-out couch. There's another that I plan on renting out. If you want it, it's yours," Buck said. "I figure, that way, if you feel like jumping off the top of it, you'll only break your arm or leg."

Stan snickered, "point taken. The trailer isn't a piece of shit, is it? Also, you're not a murderer or something weird?"

"Nah, it's nice." Buck pulled out his phone and showed Stan photos. "Also, I'm black, and we don't just kill for nothing. That's your people."

"That's nicer than my apartment. I'm gonna miss my air

mattress, but I think I can manage. Come on, there are black crazy people too; we aren't the only ones that go off the deep end." Stan handed him back his phone.

"I was just watching Harlem Nights on that big-ass TV."

"Harlem Nights?" Stan asked.

"Are you serious? You don't know what Harlem Nights is? With Eddie Murphy?" Stan maintained the look of confusion.

"See, I can't have you out here like this. Let's pack this stuff up and head on over so you can see it." Buck didn't waste any time. He got up to his feet and cleaned up after himself. "Oh… and I'm not a neat freak, but I do like a clean environment. The spot is too small to live like slobs."

"Ugh, I don't know how I'm gonna move my stuff. I'm not the best at picking up after myself, but I'll try."

"Don't worry about that. I pull my trailer with my Ford 450. I'll help you out."

Stan let out a breath of relief: "I don't know if this is a good idea, but I don't have much of a choice. I hope this works out."

"We'll be alright. I'm not a psycho or no stuff like that. You're safe. Are you a psycho? I mean other than the whole suicide stuff?"

" I'm not an axe murderer and I don't do any illegal drugs other than weed."

"Cool, we're gonna get along just fine. Let's stop in one

of these liquor stores and head back. You're gonna get fucked up, watch this movie, and then we're gonna worry about the future."

"Alright, let's do it."

Within a half hour they were back at the trailer. Buck watched Stan's face as they entered the trailer and laughed.

"You can't look scared man, the people around here smell fear. If you can make it here, you can make it anywhere. Stop looking like a mark," Buck warned him as he closed the door.

"I didn't know it was in the hood. Not that I have any problems with the hood, but dude, I'm white." Stan threw up his hands.

"White people live in the hood too, you just can't act scared. Treat people the way that you want to be treated, and you'll be fine." Stan nodded quickly and stood up straight.

"Alright... I'm going to make this work. Especially since the inside of this place looks even better than the pictures. This is brand new? I thought that you were bullshitting me with those photos. I figured you pulled them directly from the website."

"Yep, it's brand new. So, what do you think?" Buck asked.

"I think that you have a new roommate. I can make this work for a while."

"Great, now let's open up these beers while I school you on some black theater. I still can't believe that you haven't seen this movie. It's a classic."

"Sorry, I've never heard of it," Stan admitted as he flopped onto the couch.

"That's okay, I have a feeling that we're going to have a lot of movie nights. Have you ever seen Coming to America?"

Stan shook his head.

"This is just terrible," Buck laughed.

CHAPTER 5

The last few days were a beautiful nightmare for Buck. He enjoyed New York, but he hadn't done much but sight-seeing. What in the hell was he supposed to do? The weight of the world pressed on his shoulders. It was difficult not to buckle under the pressure. Stan was fully moved in and was great to have around for company. The extra income was nice, but it was New York. That money wouldn't stretch very far.

Buck lazily rolled over on his back on the full-size bed and stared at the ceiling. The light murmuring of the TV through the door greeted him. Stan was awake and watching the news. His hand reached for his phone automatically. Six text messages. Well, one text message that was just long as hell from his mom. Buck spent the last few days skillfully avoiding calls from her. He'd spoken to her a few times, but was very short with her and faked as if he were busy. His luck was short-lived, as you could only avoid Rhonda for so long.

Usually his mother didn't get under his skin; he'd been

ignoring her for quite some time. She would yell at him and accuse him of not listening. She was right. This time it was different, though. His stomach plummeted and clenched as he read all about how she was trusting him to do the right thing. *Damn, why does she have to fuck with me today? Can I just live?*

Buck loved his mom, but she could nag a man to death. Sometimes he wondered if that was the final nail in his dad's coffin. Rhonda never seemed happy, even when his dad was alive. She was sullen and complaining about patients all the time. There was no use in avoiding the inevitable.

His thumb tentatively swiped over his phone and pulled up his mom's number. The phone rang and he considered hanging up on the second ring, but it was too late.

"Boy, where in the hell have you been?"

"I've been here in New York, just figuring everything out." Buck took a deep breath and prepared himself for the lecture getting ready to come his way.

"I don't know why I expected anything different from you. You're not going to change just because your location changed. Is everything okay? Do you need to bring your butt back home? You're not getting into drugs and shit, are you?"

"Yeah Ma. I'm good. Everything is going good." Buck

closed his eyes and sighed. There wasn't any point in getting upset. He'd brought it on himself by not talking to her sooner.

"Mhmmm. I've been worried about you. I hardly hear from you. Did you ever consider that I may miss you? You're my only son, and you moved to a city where we don't know a soul. What the hell is wrong with you?"

There it was, the big heaping mound of guilt he was so accustomed to. When Buck moved into his own apartment, his mom showed up practically every day for two months until he put his foot down. He moved so that he wouldn't have to see her every day. She didn't terrorize his sister like this. Then again, his sister got married at 17 and moved out the house. He couldn't blame her, even if he did miss her at the time.

"I'm sorry I've been avoiding you. I ran into some snags and didn't want to tell you because I knew you would lose your mind over it."

"What's wrong?" she said as her voice rose a few octaves. "I knew something was wrong. I knew I shouldn't have let you go up there by yourself. What do you need?"

"I don't need anything. I need you to calm down and let me handle things. Don't worry about me. I'm a grown man, I don't need you trying to fix everything. Let me handle it." He pleaded. Talking to her raised his damned blood pressure. He wondered how she could be so cool with patients one minute and then a sporadic mess when it came to her family.

"Boy, shut up. Now, tell me what's wrong."

"Ma-"

"Don't you "ma" me," her tone mocked his. "Just tell me what's wrong. I knew it..." she sucked her teeth.

"It's not that big of a deal. The land just isn't what I expected it to be, that's all."

"What do you mean?"

"It's in the hood."

"What do you mean in the hood?"

"Like, in the projects."

"Oh, hell no! So, where have you been staying? Anybody try to rob you? You can't be down there in the fuckin' hood. You don't know shit about the hood. Did they steal your Jordans? I heard that's what they do down there. You keep your ass out of it. Sell that damned land and come home." Her instructions were quick; she said it in all in one breath.

Buck remained silent and tried to think of a way to get her off the phone. This is why he didn't want to tell her. She thought he was fragile and a punk. Whenever he had problems at school, telling her was out of the question because she would come up to the school and start problems. The last thing a boy needed was his momma coming to a school to fight his battles.

"Do you hear me, Buck? I said, bring your ass home. Do you need me to send you some gas money?" She invaded his thoughts.

"I don't need you to do anything for me right now. I'm not leaving." Buck's voice hardened.

"Oh really? So, what? You found a job or something?"

The knowing tone in his mom's voice felt like alcohol on a festering wound. She knew him, way too well. Of course, he hadn't found a job and hadn't thought that far. His account was still padded from the money she sent him with and money from his savings. She also sent him to New York with two credit cards he hadn't used yet. Hell, he didn't need a job. Jobs were for folks that didn't have funds. For now, he had one roommate and would find another soon. Job? Why?

"I know what I'm doing. I got this. I don't need you trying to make me come home. I appreciate everything you've done for me, but now I just need you to trust me. If I need to come home, I know where home is."

The phone was silent for a few moments. Buck looked at the phone to make sure his mom hadn't hung up on him.

She sighed heavily, "Alright, I just want to make sure you're doing okay. Answer my damned calls and check in more. You're grown, but I will still come up there and whip that ass."

"Don't hurt me too bad, ma," he chuckled.

"See, you think I'm playing. You think I won't go New York on your ass?" The humor in her voice shined through.

Finally, they were back in the territory where Buck felt comfortable. The part where they could laugh and enjoy one another, where she wasn't trying to run every aspect of his life.

"I know, you were gangsta back in the day."

"And don't you ever forget that. I'm about to get out of here and go to work. I wanted to call you to see how you were doing because I miss you." The relief in her voice seeped through the phone.

"How many times do I have to tell you? You don't have to worry about me. I'm going to be alright. I'll do better with callin' you and stuff. I love you."

"I love you too. I'll call you tonight."

"Wait you ain't gotta-" finishing the sentence was pointless because his mother was already gone.

"Damn," he groaned. *Now I gotta talk to her ass tonight. I ain't in the mood for all that.*

Buck laid back on his bed. He considered watching a moving and chilling out for the rest of the day. His stomach demanded to be acknowledged. He headed to the bathroom first and saw Stan watching Friday After Next.

"Enjoying yourself?" Without waiting for an answer, he closed the door to the bathroom. Stan got addicted to black movies within the short few days he'd been at the trailer.

He couldn't get enough of watching them.

Buck took a leak, washed his hands, and stared at himself in the mirror. *Damn, I look rough. I need to find a barber ASAP.* His hair and lining never took long to make an appearance. He scratched his scruffy face. He played around with the idea of growing his beard out like Rick Ross, but thought better of it.

"Have you eaten?" Buck asked when he walked into the kitchen area.

Stan shook his head, "Nope, I'm having beer for breakfast."

"Damn, dude. Ain't it too early to drink?"

"Nope, it's never too early." Buck was going to protest, but a beer with his breakfast sounded like a pretty good idea.

"Well, I'm making French toast and eggs. I'm gonna make your ass some too and then we're gonna have beer with our breakfast. You gotta eat man."

"You sound like my grandmother," Stan laughed.

"Nah, I sound like my mom. It's weird as hell, so I'm gonna shut up now, but your ass is gonna eat something."

CHAPTER 6

So many people. Keeping to your side of the street was important; Buck learned that quite a few times. When you don't, you run into people. When you run into people, that's a problem. People don't like to be touched. It didn't take a rocket scientist to figure that out. It only took a few hostile encounters.

Buck and Stan walked down the street in search of a Barber shop. Buck couldn't go another day without getting a hook up.

"Oh Lord, now you have a friend?" Buck heard a voice say from behind him. It was familiar, smooth.

He turned to see Shante. She looked even better than she did the day he saw her. She wore her braids loose around her shoulders, her make up looked good, and his attention was on her red lips. Today she didn't wear street clothes, just a black suit. The blazer hugged her curves. The pencil skirt went down to her knees and showed the world she was blessed in all areas. It took a minute for Buck to remember that he was annoyed by her. The last time he saw her, she was laughing at him and treating him like some sort of loser.

"Wassup?" he asked.

"Nothin', was just surprised to see you out here. Who is your friend?" she asked.

"This is Stan, my roommate."

He expected her to laugh and make an ignorant remark. Instead, she surprised him. "It's nice to meet you, Stan. It's good to know that Buck here isn't all alone in that trailer."

Stan gave her a huge grin. It was the grin from a man who liked what he saw. Buck gritted his teeth and steered the conversation back to him.

"So, what are you doing out here?"

"I'm getting off work and am about to take my butt home. I need sleep."

"Where do you live, anyway?" Buck took a step towards her. He wanted to be closer.

Shante gave a knowing smile and pointed down the street. "My mother lives in the building down the street. I don't live around here. I live about 20 minutes out." She pointed in the opposite direction from where he expected. "I've been trying to get her to move with me, but she refuses to let that raggedy place go. I grew up over here, and she needs a serious upgrade."

The concern for her mother rattled something inside of Buck. It was a feeling he knew all too well. Growing up, he

BUCKFOOLZ

was always worried about his mom. When his dad was alive, he worried about her, and when his dad passed away, he was more worried. Sometimes he wasn't sure which way was better. There was a part of Buck that hoped things would get better once his dad was gone. It was a thought he never outwardly expressed.

"You know moms, you can't make them do a damned thing. They're too busy trying to get you to do shit." Buck laughed in attempts to lighten his own mood.

"Don't I know it. She's still trying to run my life but I don't play that. I'm all the way grown, so she has to get over it."

"Yeah, but how can you say that if she's still paying your bills?" Buck raised an eyebrow.

Shante laughed, "Boy, please. My momma ain't paid my bills since I left her house at 18. Shit, when I lived there, I was paying some of the bills. I still do, every now and then. I take care of myself."

"How old are you?"

"Why?"

"I'm just asking. I want to know."

"I'm 24, nosy. How old are you?"

Buck shifted nervously. She was only 24, and she managed to take care of herself in New York. He was damned near 30 and his mom still paid most of his bills. What was it like to have to be self-sufficient at such an early age? He admired Shante even more. It was easy to write her off as a ghetto chick, but anyone who could do just fine in the environment she was in, had a lot more going on.

"I'm 28, I'm gonna be 29 next month."

"Awww shit, what are you doing for your birthday? You going back to Bumpkin, Georgia?" She crossed her arms and snickered.

Stan laughed and quickly covered his mouth. Buck forgot Stan was there for a moment and gave him a playful warning stare. "See the two of you think I'm funny. I'm from Lumpkin Georgia. It ain't not such thing as Bumpkin and nah, I'm not going home for my birthday. I'm going to be right here. You gonna celebrate with me?"

"Maybe I will. It depends on what you want to do."

"You probably want to have me in the clubs or something. Maybe you can tell me where I should go."

Shante shook her head, "I don't club, not anymore. I stopped around 22. Once you have been to one you've been to them all. I like restaurants and lounges. Clubs are too damned loud, expensive, and filled this thirsty-ass men."

"I thought you would like thirsty men being after you."

Her displeasure was made evident with a roll of her eyes. "I don't like parched men all in my face. I know I look good. They all just wanna screw and I'm not a damned pin cushion. The last time I went to a club, I got kicked out. A dude squeezed my ass and I punched him in the face."

"Uh oh." Buck covered his face and bobbed and weaved like a boxer. "We've got Shante Mayweather over here."

She sucked her teeth, "Boy whatever." Shante turned her attention to Stan, "Are you letting Buck drag you around the city? What in the hell are you doing hanging out with him anyway?"

"Damn." Buck grabbed his chest as if he'd been punched. "You make it sound like I'm a bad influence or something. All we've been doing is drinking and watching movies."

"Mmmhmm," Shante replied.

Deja vu struck Buck like lightening. It was his mother. Shante reminded him of his mother. It was endearing and scary at the same time. She gave him a hard time and challenged him. Did he want to be bothered? After thinking about it for a moment, a huge hell yeah screamed in his mind.

"Well," Stan chimed in, "we're just walking around right now. Buck needs to find a Barber, and I have to admit, I can't help him much in that area. Do you have any leads as to where he can go?" Shante looked Buck up and down.

"Yeah, you do need a barber. You can go around this corner to Fresh Cuts and Marlon will hook you up. He can hook the hell out of a line up."

Buck scratched his face and felt the stubble, musing,

"you sure? I don't need anyone messin' me up."

Shante's laugh cut him off. "Boy bye, your lining is already jacked up. If anything, you need him to fix it and stop trying to do it yourself."

"I don't do my linings myself. I have a barber back home."

"Well, he needs to be taken out back and shot because it's all over the place. Your lining is crooked."

"No, it's not."

"Don't argue with me, I know these things. I know a crooked lining when I see one. Just go get it fixed and tell him I sent you. He's like family."

She had a smart mouth. Who in the hell did she think she was? There was no reason for her to go in on his lining like that and his shit wasn't crooked. He'd gone to the same barber since he was 16. Insulting Larry pissed him off. Yeah, he was old as hell and his eyesight wasn't the best but he'd been in the game for a long time.

"So, you gonna go or not?" she asked.

"Yeah, I'm gonna go. He better be as good as you said."

"And if he's not? What are you gonna do?"

"I'm going to pay you a visit." Buck raised his eyebrow.

"Hmmm, I'm not sure if that's a threat or not." She bit her bottom lip suggestively.

Buck took a deep breath to keep him body from embarrassing him. The way she bit her lip made him want to see what else she could do with those full lips. "It's not a threat sweetheart. I'm just sayin' that I'll be coming to you if I don't like it. Then I'm gonna tell everybody you did it."

She laughed, "You'll be fine. After you're finished, maybe we can go shopping. Wearing white T-shirts and jeans everyday ain't cool. You don't have any clothes?"

"These are clothes."

"No, that's an undershirt you're wearing. You also need a better belt. Why are your pants so damned low?"

"I've always worn my pants like this. Ain't nothing wrong with my pants. Why are you tripping?"

She shrugged, "I'm just trying to help you out." Shante pulled her phone from her purse and grimaced, "I gotta go."

"Your man waiting at home for you or something?" Buck couldn't help but ask.

"Is that your way of asking me if I have one? If you must know, I'm single and I like it that way."

"Do you?"

"Sure do. I have less problems this way, and I can focus on what's important."

"What's important?"

"Work and school."

"Working on your Bachelor's degree? In what?"

"I'm working on my MBA."

"Oh, well excuse me."

"You're excused. I'll see you later."

"Can I get your number?" Buck asked quickly.

"Do what I tell you to do and maybe you will." She walked away.

"What does that even mean?"

"You'll find out... maybe."

Stan chuckled, "That's a spitfire."

Buck shook his head, "that's a fuckin' problem."

"You seem to like problems."

"I can't argue with you there. What in the hell was she talking about?"

Stan shrugged, "Women are complicated. You'll see her again, she's enjoying messing with you."

"You think so?"

"I know so." Stan laughed.

"I'm gonna head around to this barbershop, you gonna come with me?" Buck waited for his answer. A white man rolling up in a black barbershop would bring him a lot of entertainment.

Stan nodded, "yeah, why not? Let's go."

CHAPTER 7

She was right. It was always tough to admit it. It was always tough for Buck to admit when a woman was spot on… probably because his mother held the truth over his head like a weapon. Buck stared at himself in the mirror and couldn't help but smile. His lining and goatee looked amazing. Now, all he had to do was find someone who could re-twist his locks in a couple of weeks and he would be golden.

"What do you think?" Marlon asked.

"This is on point," Buck laughed in disbelief. "They don't cut like this where I'm from."

"You from the South, right?" Marlon asked.

"Yeah, how you know? Is it my accent?" Buck asked.

"Yes and no. Shante called me and let me know to expect you, and she told me to hook you up because you're new here." Buck smiled as he fished for his wallet from his pocket.

"Nice. I gotta make sure to thank her the next time I see her. I don't know when that will be, she didn't give me her number."

"Don't worry, I got you, bruh." Marlon grabbed a business card, wrote something on the back of it, and handed it to Buck. "This is her number. She said to give it to you if you showed up today."

"Wow, that girl." Buck plucked the card from his hand and shook his head. Trying to get next to her was like going on a scavenger hunt.

"You have no idea, dude. Shante is something else." Marlon gave him a knowing look.

It didn't occur to Buck to be jealous until then. Had he and Shante dated before? She said he was like family, not actually family. "Have you two ever been involved?"

"When we were kids, yeah. We dated but it never went anywhere. We called ourselves boyfriend and girlfriend. She and I are better off as friends." Buck tried to hide his disdain. That wasn't reassuring to hear. Maybe the two of them would pick up where they left off every now and then. It was clear he still felt something for Shante, all of it felt strange.

"Don't worry about me," Marlon said, "she and I will never be together and we don't mess around or anything like that."

"Why not? What happened, if you don't mind me askin'…" Buck cringed on the inside. He was sounding like an insecure boyfriend, and he'd just gotten her number. It wasn't any of his business about what happened between him and Shante, and he knew it. His curiosity still won, after all, Marlon was a good looking dude. He was team light-skinned, with a low-cut fade. He was put together and one of the few men wearing dress shoes in the barbershop.

"I don't mind you asking. When I was 18, I finally decided to keep it real with myself. I like men. Don't get me wrong, I like ladies too, but I like men more." Marlon's voice was low so that the other people in the shop couldn't hear him.

Buck almost choked on his spit. Out of all the things he expected to hear, that wasn't one of them. Dude was gay. Well, not gay, but damned near gay. Now the man's appearance completely made sense. "Oh."

Marlon laughed. "Is there a problem with that? I know some men don't want a barber touching them who's gay. It's not a disease you can catch and I don't push up on clients."

"Nah, it's not like that man. As long as you're cool, I'm cool."

"Don't worry, I'm not gonna fondle you or no shit like that. I keep it professional. Besides, you're not my type."

Buck tried not to take offense. "What's your type?"

Marlon laughed, "ole white chocolate over there." Buck howled with laughter when he saw Marlon nod towards

Stan. Stan looked confused as he ripped his attention away from the television.

"Stan, we're getting ready to get up out of here man."

"Make sure you call Shante today. She will nix your ass if you try to act like you're not interested. She's fickle. I'm surprised she wanted me to give you her number. She treats the shit like it's the holy grail." Marlon schooled him as he counted out the money that Buck handed to him.

"So, I'll see you soon?"

Buck nodded, "most likely next week. My hair grows pretty fast. Do you know somebody that can re-twist locs?"

"Shante knows how. Ask her and maybe she'll do it for you. She used to re-twist hair as a side hustle in college. She's really good, too."

"Thanks for the heads up. I'm going to call her today."

"Good luck... and don't hurt my friend, then you're gonna have to answer to me."

"I got you. I'm not like that."

"Okay," Marlon replied, "let's keep it that way." Buck tried his best not to skip out of the barbershop. He had Shante's number. She made him jump through a hoop for it but it was worth it.

"What's got you in such a good mood?" Stan asked.

"I got Shante's number. The barber gave it to me."

"Oh, that's what she meant then." Stan laughed, "You better be careful with that one. You sure you can handle her?"

"Yeah, I'm sure I can. She talks a good game, but we'll see. Women start out all mean and shit and then when they fall for you they're chasing you around."

Stan shook his head, "I wish. I've had more than my fair share of evil bitches. They started out nice but after we were together, they turned into the spawn of hell."

"Is that what happened with your ex-wife?" Buck asked.

Stan nodded, "Yeah she was bitch, but she only wanted to spend time with me. So that made her complain more, which made me work longer hours. Neither of us was ready to be married, I had no idea what I was getting myself into."

"Would you get married again?"

Stan thought about it for a moment. "I honestly don't know. It depends on the woman. We would have to date for a long time, I'm talking about years. I'm not going to rush back into marriage."

They walked along the streets and continued their conversation. Buck felt like a brand-new man with his fresh line up. "So how long did you date your ex-wife before you got married?"

"We dated for 6 months and planned our wedding in 3 months. We stayed married for about a year and a half."

"Damn. You two didn't waste any time, did you? That's how folks down south do it. Was she pregnant or something?" Buck didn't see the logic in marrying someone so soon unless the chick was pregnant. At six months, you barely even know her. Around that time, you both are still pretending to be great people who have it all together.

"Nope, she wasn't pregnant. We wanted to be together, and neither of us wanted to wait. We loved each other; that was all that mattered to us. Our families thought we were crazy, but we didn't care. We had a small wedding and invited like 30 people."

Buck felt sorry for Stan, he could see that it still tore him up inside. "One day you may meet a woman that's going to turn your life upside down again. You'll probably get married in 3 months or less."

"Don't curse me like that."

Buck laughed. "Say I'm wrong. You seem like the type to fall for a chick real easy."

"I know what I like." Stan defended himself.

"See, I know you."

"Fresh mangoes today," an Asian man called out. Buck's stomach growled as they approached the fruit stand. He wasn't the only one because there was an Indian man who looked to be in his mid-twenties who was practically molesting the fruit. Buck watched as he slowly inhaled the scent of the peach.

"Dude, I think you need to buy it dinner first," Buck joked.

The man turned around and laughed, "It is dinner. Well,

it's going to be lunch, I'm starving."

"Believe me, I understand. I'm hungry as hell, and this fruit is smelling too good. I don't think I've ever smelled it as strongly as I do right now. I shouldn't have waited so long to eat." Buck picked up a mango and gave it a slight squeeze. It was ripe and ready to be eaten immediately.

"Now who is making love to the fruit?" Stan joked.

The Indian man laughed, "yeah, we're making fruit look very inappropriate."

"Okay... we're gonna have to change the subject before ladies come around." Buck looked around to make sure women weren't staring at him as he molested the fruit.

"You're right. I'm Hadji by the way, it nice to meet the both of you."

Buck shook his hand. "I'm Buck."

"I'm Stan. It's nice to meet you."

"It's nice to meet the both of you. Just so you know, I usually don't go around molesting fruit. I just got off work not too long ago, and now I have a crazy appetite."

"Where do you work?" Buck asked.

"I clean pools."

"Who has a pool around here?"

"You would be surprised," Hadji laughed. "But it's in Roslyn, about 40 minutes from here. I drive out there."

"Oh, nice. Do they make you wear them little-ass pool boy shorts?" Buck asked.

"No, but my client has suggested it. She's something else."

"Oh word? I was joking. So, women really try to get at the pool boy? Is she married?"

"She's not married, but I am. My wife is back home in India. I'll be glad when I can bring her over."

"How long have you been married?" Stan asked.

"Only for a couple of years. We've known each other since we were kids."

"That's what's up. What are you up to for the rest of the day? Do you live around here? I've just moved here and I'm checking out the sites."

"No plans. Going home to get some rest."

"Oh okay, cool. You can hang out with us if you're interested in staying awake a little longer. I don't know many folks here."

Hadji looked them over and seemed to consider it.

"Are you all going to buy something or just stand here?" The fruit stand owner said.

Buck looked up at the name on the stand, "Are you Mr. Nam?"

"Yes. You buy or you go?"

"I'm sorry, we didn't mean to block your stand. We're going to buy something."

The owner gave a head nod and smiled, "okay. What do you want?"

They all paid for their fruit and walked off together.

"Honestly, I don't really feel like hanging out much. I'm ready to just get sit down and get some rest." Hadji admitted.

"No worries, you can just come by the trailer and hang out. You'll like it. We can pick up some beers and watch some movies." Buck said matter-of-factly.

Hadji's eyebrow raised, and Stan laughed. "You have to excuse Buck. He's from Georgia and overly-friendly. He's not a murderer or anything. If you want to hang out, cool, if not we understand. Right now, we're just two pathetic men wandering through life."

"I'm not pathetic," Buck said, "just jobless."

"Did the two of you say beer?" Hadji asked.

"Yep," Buck said.

"I'm in. I could use a drink."

CHAPTER 8

Buck looked around the store in awe. The walls were pink and everything was neatly organized. He almost didn't walk inside of the store, but a literal push from Shante helped do the trick.

"They do HIV testing in here, too?" Buck whispered.

Shante laughed, "Boy, why are you whispering? We're all grown in here... and yes, there's free HIV testing in here."

"I can't believe you got me in here. The walls are pink! I can't be in here."

"Oh." Shante looked disappointed.

"What's wrong?"

"I thought you would like pink walls."

Buck blinked for a few seconds and squirmed. "Well, I like those kinds of walls. I just... never mind."

Shante laughed. "Don't let it bother you. This place is amazing. This thrift store is all about giving everyone access to affordable resources when it comes to HIV, AIDS, and STDs. Everything you spend here will go to a good cause."

"Yeah, I get that, but the name is Out of the Closet. Does that mean they're mainly for..."

"The LGBT community? Do you have a problem with that?"

"No, I don't have a problem with that. I guess I just want to know what I'm getting myself into." Buck shifted nervously as a thin man with pink Justin Beiber hair walked in. He didn't have anything against gay dudes, but he wasn't used to being around so many, either. Were they looking at his ass? What was he supposed to act like, cool?

"You don't have to be gay to shop here," she laughed. "Don't worry, it won't rub off on you. The clothing selection here is pretty fly for men, and I know you're on a budget, so we're going to hook you up and be nice to your bank account. Cool?"

She sounded so confident, it put him at ease. "Yeah, that's cool. Don't have me out here in pants that look like leggings. I like to let the boys breathe."

"Oh hush, I'm going to hook you up."

Buck watched as Shante walked towards the clothing, fully expecting him to follow. He took Marlon's advice to call, and it paid off. The last two days were a huge success, even if he didn't have a way to make money. He was on a fake date with Shante and Hadji was now his second roommate. When she said he needed to get new clothes, he jumped at the opportunity to be taken shopping.

Luck struck him; when Hadji saw his trailer he went insane. He was impressed with how nice it was. She jokingly asked him if he could move in. When Buck said yes, they all had a conversation. Apparently, Hadji was fed up with his current month to month situation in a shared apartment with three other people he didn't like. He had a slumlord who didn't want to fix anything. They headed back to his place the following morning and picked up his things.

"See now, this shirt is nice." She held up a jean shirt with pockets.

Buck shook his head, "I ain't trying to look like a cowboy."

"See, this is why you can't pick out your own clothes. You don't know what the hell is going on in the world. Jean shirts are on trend and you won't look like a cowboy. There is more to the world than t-shirts and Jordans. Step your game up. You're trying on this damned shirt, and this one." She held up a red short-sleeve button down.

"What have I gotten myself into? What size is that shirt, anyway? A damned medium?"

"It's one that fits. I bet that t-shirt you have on is a 2X. Why in the hell are you wearing a shirt that damned big?"

"How did you know what size my shirt was?" he asked.

"I took an educated guess. Now come on and let's find you some jeans, too."

"I better be getting a date with you after this."

"What do you think I'm dressing you for?" she winked.

"Awww shit, let me be quiet then."

"Mhmm, that's what I thought. What are you doing on Saturday?"

"You asking me out?"

Shante sucked her teeth, "You gonna tell me or nah?"

"I don't have any plans. Damn, you ain't gotta get all forceful and shit."

"I don't feel like being the third wheel at a get together this weekend. You wanna come with me?"

Buck nodded, "I'm down. What is it?"

"It's an art exhibition; one of my friends is being showcased."

"I definitely want to go with you, but why didn't you invite one of your lil' friends to come with you?"

"They're not my lil friends. They're grown women even though they don't act like it sometimes. I love em', but sometimes they get on my nerves. Having you there will be fun. Besides, Lexi will be busy because it's her event. The other girl you saw was just an acquaintance, really. Marlon will be coming but he won't be alone."

"So, who is Marlon bringing?"

"His boyfriend, Red." She continued to focus her attention on the racks of clothing as she spoke, carefully deciding if she wanted to add it the growing pile of clothes that hung over her arm

"He has a boyfriend?"

"Yeah, why?"

"Oh, he was checking Stan out. I didn't think he was with anybody."

"Marlon is bisexual...well, gay...shit, I don't know. Whatever the case, he's a man and he still ain't shit. So that means he's still gonna look and flirt. He knows better than to let Red catch him because that will be his ass."

"Enough said then. It will be a nice little double date then. I don't have to wear a tux or no shit like that, do I?" Buck took the clothes from her arm.

"Nope, this is really low key and casual. Lexi is an Urban Artist, so this is really informal. The best part is free champagne."

"I'm not really a champagne drinker."

"Did you hear the part about free or nah?" She looked at him like he'd lost his mind.

"I guess, I'll learn."

"Smart man."

"I know how to be quiet when I'm supposed to."

"We'll see about that." A mischievous glint in her eye made Buck nervous.

"Why are you looking at me like that?"

"Because I want you to go to the dressing room and try this stuff on. While you're in there, I'll look for more stuff. I want to see everything, so don't hold out on me."

Buck tried to keep his excitement at bay. She was so damned bossy and it turned him on. "Yes, Massa."

CHAPTER 9

"Wake up," a voice whispered.

Buck groaned and turned over.

"Buck, wake up."

A frustrated grunt was all Buck could muster. He opened his eyes to see who in the hell was bothering him so early in the morning. He awoke to Hadji standing over him with a panicked expression on his face.

Buck grabbed his phone and looked at the time. "Dude, it's like 5:30 in the morning. What in the hell do you want?"

"I need a ride to work, do you think you'll be able to take me? I have to be there by 7 o'clock."

"Damn man. I thought you drove there."

"Yeah, but I rent one of those temporary cars by the hour. I'll give you gas money."

"You can't call one of those Ubers or something? You had to wake me up out of my sleep?"

"Sorry to wake you." Hadji turned and headed back to the front of his trailer.

What in the hell is wrong with that dude? Buck wondered.

Who wakes a man out of his sleep that early begging for a ride? If he wanted a ride, he should have asked him the night before. Buck tried to return to the sleep that treated him so well before he was rudely interrupted. Then the guilt sat in. Hadji sounded so damned pitiful. Buck tossed and turned a few times as he heard his new roommate getting ready for work. Eventually, he gave up and slapped his hands against the bed. "Damn."

He rose and walked to the door, "How long does it take to get to your job?"

"About 40 minutes."

"Aight, give me a minute to get dressed, and we can get out of here."

"Thank you so much."

"Yeah, it's whatever man. Just make sure you ask me ahead of time. I don't like surprises and I need to know if I'm gonna have to get up really early."

"I understand. If I need a ride again, I'll say something sooner."

Buck had the feeling that he was now the designated driver. He wanted to be mad about it, but Hadji was the only one of them who had a damned job. He needed to make sure he could keep the damned job.

"You comin' right back?" Stan asked as he rubbed the sleep out of his eyes.

"Why? You gonna miss me or something?"

Stan gave a raspy laugh, "I'm just asking. I'm going to follow up on a few connections today, so I may not be here when you get back. I have a contact that may need my assistance on some projects."

"Oh, okay. If I don't catch you then, I'll catch you later. Make sure your ass eats something."

"Yeah? Like what? We don't have any food."

"There's left over pizza in the fridge." Stan nodded. Hadji and Buck headed out the door and on their way. The view went from lively to quiet and rural.

"This is a nice area. It kinda reminds me of home," Buck smiled. As they drove, he saw animals. His stomach growled reminding him of just how hungry he was. He pulled up to a beautiful, brick home that looked like a mini-mansion. He honestly thought it would be a lot larger, but he was living in a trailer, so who was he to judge?

"This is it," Hadji said with a sigh.

"Damn, dude, you sound kind of sad. Are you gonna be alright?"

"Yes, I'm going to be fine. It's just always the same thing with her. I work hard just to do my job. She's always trying to feed me and liquor me up."

Buck frowned. "That sounds like a pretty good gig to me. I wish someone would do that for me."

Hadji shook his head quickly, "You don't understand. She's trying to sleep with me."

"Okay?" Buck didn't see the problem. "She's going to pay you, feed you, give you liquor, and offer you some ass too? Where do I sign up? Does she need a gardener or something because I need job and that one sounds like it has a lot of perks."

"I'm married," Hadji practically hissed. His mortified facial expression made Buck howl with laughter.

Buck didn't think Hadji was the kind of man who would cheat on his wife, but you never knew. Besides, his wife wasn't even in the same country. Did it count? A man has needs, Buck thought. A woman couldn't expect him to hold back when she wasn't even in the same damned country. It couldn't be him, because his wife would be severely disappointed. Long distance relationships just don't work.

"I know you're married. I'm sorry man, didn't mean to make you mad. I'm just saying..."

"Good Morning!"

Buck turned his attention towards an ugly blonde who tried to make up for it with an expensive nightgown and makeup. Buck looked at the time on his dashboard. It wasn't even 7 o'clock yet, and he could see the woman's makeup from his truck. He could see the wrinkles, too. He took back everything he thought before. She would have to pay him a shit load of money to sleep with her. Could he even get it up if he needed to?

"See what I mean?" Hadji whispered.

"Good luck, man. I wouldn't wish her on my worst enemy. Stay strong and don't drink anything she gives you. She probably will try to drug you or something." Buck felt concerned.

"I didn't think about that. You're right. I'll be careful. Thanks for the ride. Do you think you'll be able to pick me up?"

"You're lucky we're cool and that I figured you'd need a ride back. What time should I be here?"

"Probably about one. I have quite a few things that need to get done."

"Yeah, I bet."

Buck started the drive back to his trailer. He looked at the clock and wondered if it was even worth it. As soon as he got back, he would have to head right back to get Hadji. They were all going to have to figure something out; playing chauffeur every time he needed to go to work wasn't gonna happen. He would need to go back to renting that car, at least a few days a week. That's the only way all of them were going to get along.

He rubbed his temple as he drove down the long stretch of highway. The view was beautiful. He pulled over on the side of the road and climbed out of the car. There were hardly any cars driving past, just the sun, grass, and gravel. It was a slice of home in New York. Who would have known? He hopped into the bed of his truck and sat. More people needed to do that. His short time in the big city taught him quickly that people don't like to just enjoy the moment. They needed to slow the hell down, sometimes.

Being successful in New York seemed to require way too much work. After talking with Shante, Buck learned she hardly had any time to breathe or rest. She filled every moment of her life like things would crumble if she ignored it for a few moments. He smiled at the thought of her. How could one chick come into his life and turn it upside down? There was no way he would have let any other woman drag him into a gay thrift store and have him in there trying clothes. He met a lot of cool people in there, too. Soon, he would be on a double date with her and then maybe he could seal the deal.

Buck's stomach grumbled again, causing him to groan. He had the money to get something to eat, but he couldn't keep using his savings and credit card to get it. He'd end up broke, with no means of income, and then he really would have to go home to his mom. Buck tried to think of a way to hustle up on some money. He didn't wanna sell socks and shit on the street. That was played. Suddenly, the quiet was no longer comforting... he wanted to go home. He got back into his truck and drove towards home. An hour in his bed would be better than nothing. He still needed some rest.

Things were forced back into focus as something jumped out in front of him. He swerved a bit, trying not to slam the breaks, and heard a disgusting thud. Buck pulled over. After catching his breath, he looked in his rear view. *Shit, seriously?* There was definitely an animal on the road behind him. He got out of the car. It was a raccoon, a dead one.

"My bad. I didn't see you." Buck didn't know why he was talking to the damned thing, but he couldn't help it. As he started to head back to his truck, he could hear his grandfather's voice in his head, "We don't waste food around here. If you kill it, you better eat it!" Buck looked around to see if there was anybody watching him. There wasn't. People casually drove by in their own worlds. He went back to his truck to get some plastic. He was about to go back to his roots of eating roadkill and wild animals. He snorted at the irony of doing it in New York.

His stomach grumbled again in anticipation as he thought about the delicious soup he was about to prepare. His grandmother made bomb soup with raccoon and taught him how to make it too. In fact, she showed him all her recipes. His sister was too bougie to make or eat it. Before going back to the trailer, he stopped at a grocery store to grab some essentials. He prayed Stan wasn't home. Everyone wasn't down with the idea of eating road kill and wild animals. He doubted people from New York would be open to the idea. They already thought he was a dumb, country bumpkin; this would only solidify their thoughts. He slowly entered the trailer with his bags and the plastic-wrapped raccoon under his arm.

"Stan?"

The trailer was blissfully quiet. He breathed a sigh of relief and quickly got to work. His mother not only hooked him up with a trailer, but she made sure his knife collection was on point, too. He loved to cook, something she instilled in him. She wanted him to go to school to be a chef, but he shrugged it off. Cooking was something he enjoyed doing for himself, and he didn't need the world judging his shit.

He pulled out his Crockpot from a corner cabinet and smiled. His mom always hooked him up with things he didn't see as essentials until after using them. After 20 minutes, he had a fully skinned raccoon. He started to make the base for his soup.

"Man, this is gone be so damned good." The craziness of his idea hit him as he cut the raccoon into chunks and put them in the pot. His soup wasn't going to be ready for at least 4 hours, and he still needed to find something to eat now. After making sure everything was good in his Crockpot, he set off in search of food. In a couple hours, it would be time for him to head back out to get Hadji, so he needed to grab something quick and catch a nap.

A couple hours later, the alarm on Buck's phone went off. The savory scent of soup wafted over to his nose, making him hungry all over again. He had to pee, add some water to the pot, and head out to get Hadji. He opened the door and saw Stan with a spoon, practically moaning as he ate the soup.

"Dude, what are you doing?" Buck asked, more forcefully than he intended. He didn't mind Stan eating what he made, he just didn't want anybody eating his Southern soul food without knowing the ingredients.

"I'm sorry, I didn't mean to eat without asking first. This just smells so good."

Buck laughed at the site of Stan in a suit, eating roadkill and loving it.

"I'm sorry to have to break this to you, but that's raccoon soup." Buck said.

"What the fuck?" Stan dropped his spoon and wiped his mouth. "Dammit, I'm gonna be sick."

"No, you're not. It's not that big of a deal. My grandparents taught me how to make it, it's good. I was hungry and figured I would get some."

"How in the hell do you even get a raccoon? Did you buy it from one of those Asian stores or something?"

"That's racist as fuck. No, I didn't get it from an Asian store. I got it off the road."

Stan visibly turned blue. "I wish you hadn't told me that.

I'm gonna die."

Buck laughed uncontrollably, "You not gone die. You're gonna be just fine, so stop it. It was good before you knew what it was, and it's good now. You ain't gotta be dramatic about it."

"That's easy for you to say."

"It sure is. Now I'm gonna get out of here and pick up Hadji."

CHAPTER 10

Hadji and Buck walked through the door to find Stan watching Belly.

"Damn, I think you're addicted to black movies now!" Buck said and laughed.

"I would like to say you're wrong, but I can't get enough of these movies. They're so dramatic... some of them are funny as hell."

"Yeah, this is a classic, too." Bucks stomach growled at the delicious scent coming from the Crockpot.

"Man, what is cooking? It smells so good. I'm hungry, so whoever made it...you have to share." Hadji headed straight for the pot.

"Oh, don't worry man. There's plenty for you," Stanley said.

Buck looked at the amused expression on Stanley's face and couldn't help but feel a little evil. I've gotta say something, he thought. "Look, man. You might not wanna do that."

"No! It's no worry," Stanley over-talked him. "I didn't eat

it all. Hadji is hungry. I don't mind sharing my portion of what you've cooked. Buck gave an insisting look, but gave up. He could use some entertainment.

Hadji, oblivious to the undertones of the conversation, already had a bowl and spoon in hand. A low guttural moan escaped from his lips as he lifted the lid of the pot and inhaled the savory aroma.

"I had no idea you could cook like this. I haven't had any yet, but I can tell it's going to be amazing. My boss always offers me food... deep down, I don't trust it. I feel like it's a trap, maybe she'll try to slip me something. She seems like the type."

"Don't worry about," Stan said. He was practically vibrating with glee. "You can trust us, we'll never steer you wrong."

Buck snickered, trying to keep it from turning into a loud guffaw. Hadji spooned out some of the delicious soup and leaned against the counter as he blew on the spoon. He lifted it to his mouth, savoring the textures and taste of it on his palate.

"This is just as good as I thought it would be. This is downright delicious." Stan howled with laughter; Buck joined him.

"What's so funny? You all didn't spit it in or anything, did you?"

"Nah, I didn't do anything like that. I would never do

something like that." Buck sobered up as the guilt hit him. He wouldn't like it if someone did that to him. He didn't play around with his food, and allowing someone to eat something they may not like if they knew what it was wasn't right.

"Can I tell him?" Stan asked.

"Yeah man." Buck gave in.

"Dude, it's raccoon soup." Stan waited for Hadji's reaction and was sorely disappointed when he didn't get what he wanted.

"Oh? That's cool. I had some a while back, I thought I recognized the texture. It's a little greasy, but really tender. This stuff is really good but-"

"But what?" Buck cut him off. Now, not liking raccoon was one thing, but insulting his food was another. "You said you liked it. Now there's a problem?"

"Don't take it so personal. I think I can really add something to it with some cloves and cumin." Before Buck could say yay or nay, he was already rummaging through the shelves. He put some spices into the pot and stirred. Stan smiled and pointed to the pot. "Let that sit for about another half hour and you're going to taste the difference."

Buck could already smell the difference. "That smells pretty good from over here. I wouldn't have thought to put that in the pot. Seems simple, but now it's giving it an extra kick." He lifted the lid of the pot and inhaled deeply. "Oh yeah, that's it."

"Just wait until you taste it," Hadji beamed.

"I'm not tasting anything," Stan shook his head in disgust.

Buck laughed and looked at Hadji. "He thought it was pretty good until he found out what it was."

"Ah, that's why you were being such a jerk?" Hadji asked.

"I figured you would completely lose your shit like I did when you found out, but I see that you don't have any sense. Don't Raccoons have rabies?" Stan asked.

"They can, but I checked for the signs. It seemed legit. Say what you want, this stuff is good. I just may get me some more." Buck shrugged.

"I think you'll like it a lot, Stan. You should give it a try." Hadji cosigned.

Buck crossed his arms and leaned back against the wall. "There is no way I'm eating that again. Fool me once, shame on me, fool me twice...can't fool me again."

"Umm, I'm pretty sure that's not how it goes," Hadji laughed.

"I know, it's one of my favorite Bushism's." Stan winked.

"I really hated Bush when he was in office, but now that we may get a certified clown in office, he's not looking so bad." Buck laughed.

"At this point, I'll take someone from an independent

BUCKFOOLZ

party." Hadji chimed in. "I think we need to start giving them more of a platform. They deserve a second look, because this two-party system is broken."

Stan groaned, "Can I finish watching my movie in peace without thinking of the future? It's pretty depressing, right now."

"I thought you had something in the works," Buck said.

"Maybe, but it won't take off for quite some time, and I don't have that kind of time. I need a change, and I need it now. I don't like being broke."

Hadji gave a knowing nod. "Don't be so rough on yourself. Things will get better. With the three of us here, maybe we'll come up with a way to make some money so I don't have to get harassed by my boss anymore."

"Ya know, you complain about that job a lot," Stand said. "It doesn't sound so bad."

"Oh, it's bad. It's real bad. I thought the same thing." Buck shook his head the entire time of talking. "That woman is scary. She looks like she sacrifices babies."

"She's not that bad," Hadji said.

"Oh, so you're sweet on her now?" Buck wondered if Hadji secretly liked the attention he got from the crypt keeper.

"Not at all," Hadji replied.

"Maybe she's just one of those single old ladies on the hunt for some young stuff."

Hadji shook his head, "No. She's married."

"Wow." Stan looked disgusted. "Trying to sleep with the pool boy? That's pretty cliché, but I guess that old story is popular for a reason. Women love to mess with the pool boy, apparently. Maybe I should apply for a job around there. I'm single and can do whatever I want."

The men sat around talking about marriage and cheating for the next half hour. Buck kept his eyes on his watch. The food was smelling so good... he couldn't wait to get a taste. When it was time, he made his way back to the pot and spooned out half a bowl. The flavors exploded on his tastes buds.

"Oh damn." He laughed. "This is so good that we could sell it."

CHAPTER 11

Buck looked in the mirror and smiled. He dug his New York swag. Tonight, he planned on getting to know Shante better and hopefully sealing the deal on their date. The clothes she picked for him were nice. He didn't want to pump her up, but he looked good. His locs were pulled back, his denim button up shirt perfectly gathered at his elbows, straight-legged jeans fitting perfect, with casual shoes.

"Damn boy, don't hurt em'," Buck said.

He stood back and did a few poses. "Nah, I need some pics." After a few bathroom selfies, he emerged.

Hadji gave an approving nod. "You look nice."

"Thanks. Gotta dress to impress, you know what I mean?"

"Have a good time."

"Where did Stan go?"

Hadji shrugged and put his tablet down on the table. He was watching some Indian movie. Buck didn't know what the hell they were saying on the screen. "He got a message on his phone and hit the road like a dog out of hell."

"I'm pretty sure it's bat out of hell..."

"What?"

Buck laughed and grabbed his wallet from the table, "the saying. It's not a dog out of hell. It's bat out of hell."

"Oh. I'm sure if dogs were down there they would leave pretty fast too."

"You have a point."

Buck pulled his phone from the holster on his side and checked it. It was a little after 7; he would need to meet Shante at the exhibit soon. "I'm gonna head out. Don't do anything I wouldn't do."

"You don't have anything to worry about," Hadji laughed.

Buck liked Hadji a lot. He was small and unassuming, but he had a lot of dignity about himself. Not a lot of people could make simple things look deep. He watched his movie like it had the keys to universe. It almost made Buck want to learn a new language. Almost.

Taking the train was an option, but Buck didn't want to risk it. The last thing he needed to do was hop on the wrong one and end up late. Instead, he walked a few blocks over and caught a cab. The place was only about 25 minutes away. The cab driver whipped in and out of traffic, flipping a few people off and honking his horn like a mad man. *Damn and people say that country folks can't drive,* Buck thought. These people were insane. When too many people were in one place, they acted a damned fool.

He looked down at his phone and saw a text from his mother. She asked him how he was doing. He groaned and rubbed his temple. His mother thought they were supposed to talk a few times a day. It was way too much for his liking, but he tried to be understanding. She missed him, and he couldn't blame her: he missed her, too. Being away from his family and friends was a huge adjustment, but he was a man. Sitting around and talking to his momma all day wasn't a good look. Instead of ignoring her like he wanted to, he texted her back to let her know he was doing alright and was on his way out for the night. That way, she wouldn't expect a lot of back and forth.

She needed friends outside of work- well, she needed better friends outside of work. The ones she had were full of drama and bad luck stories, and they always needed something. Their son was in jail and needed bail money, or they didn't have any food in their house. His mom talked a lot of crap and always claimed she wasn't going to give people things, but everyone knew she was soft. They may have to hear her mouth off for the next few months, but she came through every time. Her job, plus the insurance money his dad left behind, turned his mom into a country bumpkin philanthropist. She had to save everybody, all the time. He told her she needed to learn how to keep her money to herself, but she always shushed him.

She always said, "Shut up. We're blessed to be a blessing. If you can't give then you don't deserve to receive." He guessed she was right. Buck never wanted for anything. His mom always took excellent care of him and his sister, even when things were emotionally rough. When his mom cooked, there were always at least two people not related to them at the table, and that's not counting his aunts, uncles, and cousins. The dinner table was packed like a restaurant. That was on the nights his mom wasn't working. His family tried to start coming on when it was just he and his sister at home, because they cooked too, but they weren't having any of that. They would avoid answering the phone and even the doors, sometimes.

"Let them in one time, and they'll think they can bring their hungry butts over here all the time. They need to learn that we're not their momma," his sister said.

See, now that was logic he could get behind. Feeding a bunch of freeloaders who never gave anything back was some bull. If he cooked for people, they were going to have to pay up. Forget the free ride; it wasn't gonna happen. Hell, he hardly had anything to give them, anyway. He was still trying to make it.

"You pay me," the African man said aggressively.

Buck looked around, "Oh, my bad. I didn't notice that we

stopped." He pulled out his wallet and paid his expensive cab fare. Gas was high, but it wasn't that damned high. He could see why people took public transportation. Riding in a cab alone was expensive. He hopped out of the cab and stared at the small, windowless, brick building. It had to be the right place: there was a doorman outside with a black velvet rope and a few people in line. He looked around for a moment to take it all in. This was one of his first nights being out on the town, in New York. Life was hard, but he could see why people loved it so much (and why entire songs were dedicated to it). The energy of everyone around him was contagious.

"Looking for me?" Someone tapped his shoulder.

Buck turned to his left and saw Shante. She smiled so brightly that he almost fell out. She looked happy to see him; he was also really happy to see her. Her box braids fell over her shoulders and framed her face. She had on makeup, but he could still tell who she was. Her full red lips made him want to kiss her.

"Yeah, I guess I was." He pulled her into a hug, and was surprised when she gripped him tightly. "It's good to see you," he whispered in her ear.

"I think I missed you a little bit," she said.

"Oh yeah, only a little bit?"

"I can't tell you a lot or you'll think I'm soft."

So... everything he felt for her was mutual. It must have

been a full moon because she was being more agreeable than he'd ever experienced. She usually had a smart mouth. He didn't mind that, but he didn't mind this version of her, either.

Someone behind them loudly cleared their throat. Shante pulled away from him. Buck tried to push back his disappointment.

"So, that's how ya'll are getting down?" Marlon said.

Buck smiled and extended his hand. "Good to see you again, man."

"Good to see you, too. We were looking for Shante. She disappeared... and here she is, being all felt up." Marlon raised his perfectly manicured eyebrow.

"Shut up, Marlon, he wasn't feeling me up. We were hugging. You can be so extra sometimes."

"She's defensive, too," the white man next to Marlon said.

It took a minute for everything to register. The tall white man was Marlon's boyfriend. It was no wonder Marlon was digging on Stanley. This was the kind of white man he saw black women falling over and wishing they had enough courage to date. He'd heard his sister and mama fawning over white men, but refused to try. They couldn't fathom dating outside their race, so they just looked and never touched.

"As you can see, I have a thing for white meat," Marlon

laughed. "My taste doesn't really vary."

"Hi, I'm the white meat." Red extended his hand.

Buck laughed. "It's nice to meet you, man. I'm Buck."

"You can call me Red."

"I'll do that, Red. Is the nickname because of the obvious, or because of something else?"

Red nodded. "I would love to say that I got the name because I'm a white boy, but no, my real name is Redcliff. I've gone by Red ever since I started school."

"Damn. Redcliff? I thought my name was bad."

"Oh, it is bad," Shante laughed.

Buck gave her a mock-warning look.

She mumbled, "I'm just saying. You wear it well, though."

"Yeah, that's what you say now."

Shante looped her arm through his and leaned her head on his shoulder. "Don't be like that. Let's get inside and look at this art before Lexi thinks none of us love her."

"Wait, Lexi? The girl I met when we first met?" Buck asked.

"Yes. Is that a problem?"

Buck tried not to frown but he failed.

Shante grinned. "Don't be like that. I know you're still not holding that little encounter against her?"

"Why didn't you tell me it was her event?"

"Because then you may not have come, and I wanted

you here with me today." She smiled sweetly.

Any resistance flooded out of him. How could he be mad at someone so fine? When she acted all sweet, it disarmed him.

Marlon and Red laughed.

"We're gonna steer clear of the both of ya'll tonight because I already see where this is headed," Marlon said.

"Where is this headed?" Buck asked.

"Shut up, Marlon." Shante pulled Buck towards the door.

Once inside, Marlon's eyes lit up. Art. Art was everywhere. The lighting hit them just right. The images were captivating. It was a mix of paintings and photography. So many faces. All of them looked like they were staring right through him.

"Nice, right?" Shante said.

"Okay, I'll admit it. You were right. Your girl has skills. I never would have expected something like this from her."

"What would you expect from me, then?" a voice said from behind him. He didn't want to turn around. He stuck his foot in his mouth; Lexi was right behind him. Freezing up wasn't manly. He said what he said, so he had to back it up. Buck turned to face her. He was struck. She looked really good, a far cry from the rude girl he'd seen when they first met. Her African print dress showed off her curves, her hair was pulled up into a bun, and her makeup was done, too.

"Well, Miss Lexi. I can call you that, can't I?"

"Oh wow." Shante snickered. "I've never seen you kiss an ass before."

"Hey, I gotta make it up somehow."

Lexi nodded. "You sure do. Yes, you may call me Miss Lexi. What did you expect from me?"

"Honestly, I didn't know what to expect. I can say that I'm shocked. This art is on some next level stuff. You've got skills."

"I would hope so. I've been going to school for this for nine years."

"Well, excuse the hell out of me."

She broke out into a laugh, showing off the gap that she wore with pride. "It's all good. It's not like I was nice to you when I first met you. You probably thought I was a hoodrat, not that I mind being called one. I am who I am."

"Not at all," Buck said too quickly.

"At least you have the decency to lie. I'm glad you made it, Buck. I'll catch up with the two of ya'll later. I gotta attend to the folks who are actually gonna buy my stuff."

Shante smacked her lips, "How you know I'm not gonna buy anything?"

"You don't have space on your walls for anything else. I think my art has taken it all up."

"I still have some space."

"Girl, bye. Your place is gonna look ratchet as hell if you

keep hanging my pictures everywhere. There is a limit, but I love the support." Lexi kissed Shante on the cheek and went to greet the other guest.

"Don't think I didn't see you looking at my friend," Shante said.

"I wasn't looking at her like that. She looks nice today. Ya'll clean up nice."

"Look whose talkin'. You're in here looking all urban suave."

"Keep sweet-talking me like that, and we're going to go on our third date." Buck said low enough so only she could hear.

"Isn't this our first?"

"No, the shopping trip was our first date."

"That was not a date!"

"I say it was."

"And why's that?" Shante took a step closer into his personal space so that others could walk past her.

"Because you took me out shopping. It was personal time we had together, so it counts in my book."

"I don't know what book you're reading from, but in my book, that's not a date."

"We're reading from my book tonight. Is that okay?"

"Hmm, I'll think about it. Let's go see what's over on the other side." She grabbed his hand and walked him towards the other side of the room where Red and Marlon were.

Buck liked being dragged around by her.

A few hours later, Buck, Shante, Marlon, Red, and Lexi sat in a restaurant and devoured the Asian fusion food in front of them. Buck was on his second California Roll. The ginger, soy sauce, and Avocado danced on his palate.

"You know that's not real sushi, right?" Marlon said before he popped a salmon and mango roll into his mouth.

Buck smirked. "What makes you say that?"

Marlon shrugged as he swallowed his over stuff mouth. "Sushi has raw meat in it. That's just an American version of something authentic. Americans love to appropriate cultures and water it down."

Buck nodded. "Interesting."

"Sorry, don't blame the messenger."

"Oh my God." Shante groaned. "Marlon, do you have to be a know-it-all about everything? We didn't need the lesson."

"What?" Marlon looked around the table in mock offense. "I'm just trying to tell Buck to step his game up. He's here in New York now and has access to a ton of new food. It may be time for him to expand his palate."

Red shook his head. "I'm sorry, Buck. Marlon doesn't know how to keep his mouth shut."

Buck laughed. "It's okay. I wasn't going to get into this, but since we're educating, I'll add my own." He cleared his throat dramatically. "The word sushi means vinegar rice.

Makizushi means rolled sushi. The California roll's invention is credited to Ichiro Mashita, a Japanese sushi chef in Los Angeles from the 1970's. Try to tell him that it's not sushi. See, the California Roll definitely has vinegar rice, and it's rolled, which means…" he smiled, "it's Mazizushi, or sushi. The only sushi form that requires raw fish is Sashimi. There are some sushi types that don't use fish at all, like Kappamaki and Futomaki."

Everyone at the table stared at him with their mouths practically gaping open.

"What in the entire hell?" Lexi laughed. "Dude, did you really just break down sushi for us? Did you really just shut down Marlon? Did you really just snatch all of our edges? In the words of Kanye, 'how'?" Lexi clapped jovially. "We have a damned food genius among us and didn't even know it. Did you see this on the Food Network, or what?"

"No, I went to culinary school for a bit. I thought I wanted to be a chef but didn't finish."

"Why didn't you finish?" Shante asked.

He shrugged, "I was over it. I only had about 3 months left and was kind of just doing it for fun. It wasn't fun anymore, so I quit. I was good at it but didn't like the food they were teaching us to cook."

Marlon rolled his eyes and leaned against Red. Lexi snickered and pointed, "Awww, you mad or nah? Didn't we tell you to stop messing wit people? Now you've sat here and got all embarrassed."

Marlon smacked his lips, "Girl please, I am not embarrassed. What is there to be embarrassed over?"

"Ummmm, you just got schooled."

Shante shook her head. "Lexi, leave him alone."

"Yes, please leave my man alone. I have to go home with him." Red kissed the top of Marlon's head. "It's okay, baby. Your heart was in the right place."

Marlon sat up and cut his eyes at everyone. "All of you can go to hell. Buck, can you make Sushi?"

Buck nodded, "Yeah. I could be better at it, but that was something we covered for a lil bit."

"I will have to see that for myself or I won't believe you."

"Didn't I just teach you a lesson about underestimating me?"

"He's just trying to get free food," Lexi said.

Buck nodded. "Oh, I know. That's why I'm not serving him any sushi. I have some soup you can try: my roommates love it."

"Oh? I'll give it try."

Buck laughed to himself. Now Marlon was one person he wouldn't feel bad about feeding a raccoon too.

CHAPTER 12

Buck walked Shante up the stone stairs to her place. It was a little past 1 am, and the evening was winding down. He didn't want it to end, but the inevitable was coming.

"Did you have a good time?" Shante asked.

"Yeah, I had a really good time. Lexi's art is dope."

"Are you going to give her number to Stan like you promised? You know she's serious, right?"

Buck nodded his head and laughed. "Yeah, my word is my bond. I don't know if Stan is ready for all that, but I'm going to do what I promised."

While out at dinner, Marlon asked Buck where his "fine white chocolate" friend was. Red looked unbothered about his mate complimenting and asking about another man. Buck was surprised; he couldn't imagine ever doing that in front of a woman he was with. If he did something like that, he would have to hide the silverware. Buck said he didn't know where Stan was. Shante cosigned on the fact that Stan was fine and Buck tried to hide his jealousy. He didn't do very well when everyone at the table laughed.

Lexi then asked if he was single, and the rest was history. Buck was roped into passing off her number to Stan.

It was going to be interesting to see if the two of them hit it off. He didn't even know if Stan was into black women. He knew that his ex-wife was a white woman. Either way, it didn't mean much to Buck. He'd be amused with whatever Stan did, so yes, he was going to keep his promise.

"Good." Shante gave a satisfied nod. "Lexi needs a man so bad."

"I can't vouch for him or anything. I've never seen what he's like in a relationship. Whatever happens with them, don't blame me. We can't let it mess up what we've got going on over here."

Shante smiled. "What do we have going on over here?"

"You tell me."

"See, there you go. You're the one who said it, so I assumed you had some kind of insight that I didn't."

"There you go assuming."

"Keep it up. Keep talking smart to me, and I may change my mind about inviting you in."

Buck nearly choked on his own spit. She was going to invite him in? There was only one thing that happened in a woman's place that late. He figured he would have to wait much longer to get to that step.

"Close your mouth. That lip is hanging and a fly may

rest in there."

"You're really going to invite me in, or are you playing?" He asked.

"Do I look like the type of woman to play around? When I know what I want, I go for it. We don't have to beat around the bush for this, unless you want to."

"No." Buck said quickly. "I'm down for getting right to it."

She leaned in and pressed her warm lips against his own. Buck inhaled her breath. So soft. Her lips were just as soft he thought they were. She pulled back from him and put her key in the over-sized wooden door. "Good."

CHAPTER 13

Buck sang a little tune as the bacon sizzled in the pan. His stomach growled in anticipation as the scent of bacon permeated the entire place. He had so much room. He could dance while he whipped up pancakes. The small stack was finally complete.

"I could get used to this," a voice from behind him said.

He turned around to see Shante standing in the doorway with an over-sized t-shirt on. It was incredibly sexy and disconcerting at the same time. That was the kind of t-shirt women took from their lovers and never gave back. Did she buy that shirt herself? Or was the blue t-shirt with the popular brand logo on it from an ex-lover? His brain was overloaded with too much information, so he decided to stop and just enjoy the view. They weren't officially in a relationship, so it was unfair to expect her to get rid of items from her wardrobe.

"I could get used to this, too." He walked away from the stove and gave her a quick peck on the cheek. "I hope you're hungry."

"I'm very hungry. We kind of worked up an appetite last night."

He smiled at the blush on her face. She was so funny to him. On the outside, she was sassy and no-nonsense, but there were more layers to her. In the bedroom, she was sweet and submissive. It shocked the hell out of him and turned him on at the same time. He felt like a conqueror.

"We did, didn't we? I had a really good time with you."

"Oh, believe me. I know. It was weird though."

"Why was it weird?"

"I'm usually never like... that."

Buck's eyebrow furrowed as he placed the bacon strips on a place covered with paper towels. "What do you mean?"

She laughed. "I'm not trying to be that girl. You know, the one who has sex on a first date and then claims she usually doesn't do that. Granted, it hasn't been something that I've done for a while, but that's not what I'm referring to. I'm talking about the way that I was with you. I'm usually the aggressor and sex for me has been...I don't know." She sighed heavily. "How about we just get to eating? I see you've found your way around my kitchen pretty well. I'm kind of impressed."

"Don't doubt my cooking skills. I was raised in the kitchen. I wanted to be a chef."

"Seems like you are a chef, to me. You don't need a degree for that."

This time it was Buck who had to hold back a blush. Having someone support his dream always got to him. They sat at her small circular table and dug into the food.

"You know I can't let you off the hook, right?" Buck said after the best of hunger was satiated and he could slow down a bit.

"What do you mean?" she asked.

"I really need to know what was so different about last night." They stared at one another in silence for a bit; the sexual tension between them was thick enough to be cut with a knife. *Damn*, Buck thought. *How is she doing this to me?* She challenged him on every level, and he needed to know everything about her. Sex with her after the first date didn't make him think any less of her. If anything, she only intrigued him more, now.

"Didn't I say we weren't going to talk about that?"

"Hey, I'm not the one who brought it up, you did. Don't blame me."

"Whatever."

They continued to chew in silence. He wondered if he should have left the conversation alone.

She groaned and hit the table with a loud smack, shaking her head. "Nope, you're not going to bring your country butt into my life and turn it upside down. I don't have time for this."

"I don't even know how I should take that."

"I don't know how to take it, either. Don't think I'm crazy or going to stalk you or anything, but the sex last night was different from anything I've ever experienced, which is weird. I felt connected. It wasn't just an act that I was doing and trying to cum, you know? I felt something. Ugh, I probably sound like one of those clingy chicks."

Buck grabbed one of her hands in his and stroked it with his thumb. "I understand what you mean, but I felt like that from when I first met you. There is something different about you, and I really like it. Last night was great. It was deep. It was the kind of sex you see in the movies. It was passion, heavy breathing, hair pulling, and all of that. Just like you, I felt something, too. Don't try to pull away from me or act all funny now that I've blown your back out."

A surprised laugh escaped her lips. "See, that's what happens when you give a man a little bit of power. He loses his mind. Don't get ahead of yourself. I will completely ruin you."

"You've already ruined me," he replied. "I don't want anybody else. I just want you."

Shante shook her head in disbelief. "Where did you come from?"

"Bumpkin, Georgia," he said.

CHAPTER 14

"Hey stranger," Stan said.

"What's up?" Buck said off-handedly as he entered the trailer.

"Don't try to pretend nothing happened. I gotta know how your night went, man."

"It went the best way it could have gone. I'm not coming back in the morning, it went bad."

"I hear ya."

"What did you end up doing last night?"

Stan ran his hand through his hair and took a deep breath.

"I didn't do a damned thing. I ignored a few calls from the ex-wife, watched some movies, that's about it."

"Why are you ignoring her calls?"

"She doesn't want to talk about anything I care about. Now she wants me back, and I can't put myself through that."

"Yeah, don't let anybody drag you through the mud. It's one thing to go into a situation where you don't know what's gonna happen. It's another when you already know what's around the corner. You've been there and done that. Move on and find somebody better."

"I feel like I'm okay without dating right now."

"Hell, no."

"What?" Stan asked defensively.

"That's some female stuff. I just want to do me right now. I just came to the club to dance with my girls. I'm going to wear a wedding ring so no one will talk to me. You better snap out of it and not let life pass you by. You've wasted enough on that chick. It's time for you to live. I may have someone for you."

"Who?"

"Shante's friend, Lexi. I thought she was just a loud mouth know-it-all and, come to find out, she's a dope artist. She was fifth-wheeling it last night. I could tell she wished she had somebody."

"I don't know."

"Is it because she's black?"

"No!" Stan said quickly. "I'm just not sure about dating and all that. If you say I should date her, then I know she's good. It's just that, when you start dating friends of friends, it can get messy and awkward if it doesn't work out."

"Damn, you haven't even met her yet, and you're already thinking about a break up? Go with the flow. We're all grown here. I think she might be just what you need. Leave those white girls alone, Stan, and get you a sister. She'll change your life." Buck took a seat at the small kitchen table. "Man, I'm hungry."

"Me too. I'm so hungry I was thinking about your roadkill soup. It was really good."

"I know, right. I've really been thinking about selling it," Buck laughed.

"I don't know why you're laughing. I think that's a great idea."

"Really? You want me to serve up some raccoon soup to the public? They're gonna execute me, man."

"They don't have to know. Shit, people think that the Chinese restaurants serve them dog and pigeon but they keep going, anyway. People want to be lied to when the food is good. The truth is they don't care as long as it's affordable, looks good, and tastes good."

Buck stared at Stan as if he'd lost his mind. "You can't be serious."

"Oh, but I am." He pulled his laptop from the edge of his bed and opened it. "I've given this some thought and even worked out some details. We just need some investments and we can get us a food truck and park it right on this lot. This neighborhood is already booming, so you'll have plenty of customers."

"Where are we supposed to get the money for something like that? A food truck? Don't we need licenses and stuff?"

"I've been looking that up, too. It's not as difficult as you think. Hadji isn't here, but I spoke to him, and he has a sanitation license. Apparently, he used to run the kitchen at some Indian restaurant and had to get it. He keeps it updated."

Buck's head started to spin. That was a crazy idea. Selling road kill to the neighborhood? Was that ethical at all? Could he go to jail for that? He wasn't sure, but he damned sure didn't want to find out.

"Stop stressing out about it, and get some rest. We can talk about later. I know you're tired as hell."

"True, I didn't get much sleep last night."

"Yeah, I didn't think so."

"So, while I'm sleeping I'm gonna need you to give Lexi some more thought. I'm telling you man, you're going to really like her."

"Why do you keep trying to push her my way?"

"I ain't trying to push her your way, I'm trying to put you on. There's a difference. I'm tired of seeing you mope around over a marriage that's over. You said you don't want your ex-wife back, so act like it. Be a man and move on to someone else. It's what you need, and she'll pull you out of your shell, too."

"How does she feel about white men?" Stan asked.

"She doesn't care. Oh, yeah! I forgot to tell you. You know Marlon, the dude that cut your hair and wouldn't stop flirting with you? You know, he has a boyfriend named Red."

"Okay, what do I need to know this information for?"

"They were there last night, and Red is a white boy. I didn't expect that all. I'd say you're off the hook, but he likes white meat, so you may wanna get you a partner before he tries to make you his side chick."

"That's not funny. I'm not a homophobe, but I don't want to be looked at like a piece of meat by one of them, either."

"I hear ya. Last night, Marlon tried to play me. I had to embarrass him in front of everyone. I think we have a mutual understanding now."

"I don't want to have any kind of understanding with him. I don't judge anyone for their sexuality, but the flirting is a little over the top for me."

"The flirting is a little over the top for you with everyone, it seems. You need a life. It's a shame I've just moved here and been on more dates than you."

"You've only been on like one date."

"Exactly." Buck threw his hands up. "That's exactly what I mean."

"Go take your nap."

"You just think about what I said." Buck walked back towards his room.

"Yeah, and you sleep on what I said."

CHAPTER 15

Buck's heart pounded so hard he felt like it was going to come out of his chest. He was taking the plunge; there was no going back. Once he put it out there, he could never say it was a mistake. Maybe he could laugh it off if people thought he was crazy? Maybe everyone would talk him out of his loony idea. If they didn't, maybe they would pitch in and help. The truth was that he needed to start making some money and build a life for himself. He did sleep on what Stan told him, and he even gave it a few weeks. The more he mulled it over in his head, the clearer things became. That wasn't such a bad idea.

Sure, there were a few things he had to do before he could take that step, but that didn't make it impossible. He moved to New York on a prayer, and he was still managing to make things happen. New York was the land of dreams and hustlers. When you wanted something, you didn't wait for it to come to you. You had to go out and get it. Waiting for money to fall into your lap was the easiest way to end up broke.

He stared at all the faces around the trailer. Shante sat at the booth in the kitchen with Lexi seated next to her. Lexi couldn't keep her eyes off Stan, who was sitting on his neatly-made bed. Stan's face was flushed red. Just like Buck thought, he liked Lexi. It was their first time meeting, and that was partially the reason he invited Lexi in the first place. Sure, she could pitch in and help on his idea, but it was time for her and Stand to meet face to face, since his friend refused to reach out. Heartbreak is a trip.

Buck wondered what exactly happened between Stan and his ex-wife; she sure did a number on him. What kind of man doesn't want to date? Men weren't supposed to take breaks and heal emotionally after relationships. You were supposed to move on to the next woman and let all that healing crap take place during the process. Really, Buck couldn't truly identify with Stan. He had a girlfriend in high school who kind of broke his heart. She left him for some fool in the next town over. She claimed it was because the guy wanted to get married. They were only 16! She wanted him to marry her and have babies before they got out of high school.

It was crazy as hell, in his opinion. Shortly after he told her that he wanted to wait to get married, she left him. One year later, she was married and already had an infant. It stung a bit, but he didn't want to switch places with the guy. Now they were four kids in, and the man was a fat, miserable cheater. He would feel sorry for her, but there wasn't any point. He probably was never going to marry her, anyway. He liked her a lot, but she was too skinny for his taste. Buck thought that, maybe after his ex had a couple of kids, she'd start to thicken up, but nope. She was still stick thin. What a shame.

"So, why are we all here?" Shante asked, pulling him out of his trance.

Hadji snickered as he leaned against the counter. "I'm interested, as well. This isn't very much like you."

"Thank you for asking. I've called you all here because I have an idea and I need to know if you all will ride with me on it or not. I'm not from here, and so I don't have a lot of people I can trust. I trust everyone in this room."

"Even me?" Lexi asked. She smacked her lips and tilted her head.

"Yes, even you, Lexi. You're crazy, but you're about your , and I like that. I'm going to need your guidance on this new venture."

"This sounds fishy. You trying to get us to push drugs or something? I'm too cute for jail." Lexi raised an eye brow.

"I agree." Stan mumbled.

"What was that?" Lexi asked.

Stan looked mortified; Buck gave him the 'speak up' look. Stan cleared his throat. "I was just agreeing with you. You're too cute for jail."

Everyone stared at Stan for a moment and then busted out laughing.

"Ya'll leave him alone," Lexi said. "The man has taste. Thank you, Stanley."

"People call me Stan."

"Well, I'm going to call you Stanley. I prefer calling everyone by their government name."

"Really, Alexis?" Shante laughed.

"Don't blame me. Everyone has called me Lexi since I was a baby. I can't control that. If people want to call me Alexis, that is okay with me. I like my name."

"Cool, then I'm going to call you Alexis," Stan said.

Stan and Alexis exchanged curious looks with one another.

"Okay, before it gets too hot on this trailer, we need to get back to the business at hand." Buck shook his head and grinned. The two of them were going to hit it off just fine. "Long story short, I'd like to do a food truck and sell food right here, on this lot. I'll be learning everything from the ground up, so I may need everyone's expertise on this. Of course, I'll share the profits."

"You have the capital to get something like this started?" Lexi asked immediately. "Also, what kind of food are you thinking about serving?"

Both of those questions were difficult to answer, and also a bit embarrassing. The quicker he came out with it, the better. If they told him no, it would be their loss because he knew the food truck was going to be a hit.

"I'm working on getting the money for the food truck, so don't worry about that. Now the answer to the second question is what's going to take more time."

"Can you hurry? My stomach is grumbling. What are in those containers on the counter? I'm hungry as hell and it smells really good in here." Lexi groaned.

"Actually, that's what I wanted to share with you. I want you to eat. Buck laced the Tupperware in front of them and took off the tops."

"Oh my god, yes," Lexi said. "This is what I need in my life. Food." She pulled the burger to her. "This one is mine."

"Lexi, you act like you've never seen food before." Shante looked at her in disgust.

"I'm not trying to front around anyone. I'm hungry as hell, and food is here. I'm going to eat."

Buck wanted to stop her and tell her that everyone was supposed to share, but her hands were already all over it. Her eyes rolled to the back of her head. "This is so good. What kind of sauce is on here? Wow." She covered her full mouth with her hand. "I'm serious. What is it?"

"See now, if I told you that, I would have to kill you." Buck laughed.

"Well if she's diggin' in, then I want to dig in, too." Shante grabbed a taco and closed her eyes in pleasure with each bite. "See, I knew you could cook, but this is on an entirely different level. Why didn't you finish school? You play entirely too much."

Shante and Lexi gave one another the thumbs up as they pigged out on his food. Stan stared at them and tried not to keep from laughing.

"Umm, is this the meat you purchased from Mr. Nam's hook up?" Hadji asked.

"It is."

"Don't you think you should say something?" Hadji had a mortified look on his face.

Shante looked confused as she swallowed a huge bite. "Say something about what?"

Hadji looked at Buck and gave him the stare of death.

"Umm, ya'll two may want to kill me after I tell you."

"Uh oh." Stan laughed.

It just hit Buck that the two women sitting in front of him may not find it as funny or be as easygoing about it as Stan was. They weren't country girls who'd eaten what their dad or uncles brought home. They didn't know anything about farm animals, so they definitely wouldn't be up for wild animals. Now, Lexi might not be that upset; the content of her burger was acceptable. Shante was going to skewer him alive once she found out what was in her tacos.

He didn't get these animals off the side of the road the

way he did the raccoon, but they were animals people didn't traditionally eat from Mr. Nam, the guy from the fruit stand. He and Mr. Nam bonded over the talk of moonshine. The week before, he made him a gallon in exchange for free fruit and vegetables. Buck quickly learned that Mr. Nam was a bit of an alcoholic. When he returned a few days later, Mr. Nam was already searching for gallon number two. Mr. Nam then gave him the number to a "friend" who farmed pets that weren't the norm.

Buck was able to get his hands on deer, squirrel, rabbit, and raccoon. He felt like he hit the jackpot. When he threw in a little extra, the meat was already cleaned and prepped for cooking. That was the route he'd need to go if he planned on selling in New York. That way, he wouldn't have to be worried about people seeing what he brought on the truck.

"This isn't a rat, is it?" Shante pushed the Tupperware container away. "Oh my god, please tell me we're not eating rats."

"No! It's not a rat," Buck said. "It's squirrel!"

"What?!" Lexi yelled, "We ate a damned squirrel?" I'm going to kill you! Oh my god, I think I'm going to be sick." She made gagging noises.

"No, you're eating deer." He told Lexi.

"Oh, but you sat here and let me eat a squirrel and you

weren't going to say anything?" Shante said with a calm that surprised Buck.

"I'm sorry. I wanted to know how you felt about it first. I knew if I told you what it was, then you would get all upset about it. It's safe."

"At least he didn't get your food off the side of the road," Stan mumbled.

"I'm gonna die. I ate Bambi," Shante put her hand to her mouth. "You're not supposed to eat deer."

"Who decided what we're supposed to eat and what we're not supposed to eat?" Buck asked. "Meat is meat, it doesn't matter what source it comes from. Come on ya'll, admit it. This food is really good, right?"

Shante shook her head, "I should slap fire from you. Who does this?" She looked at the container that still contained two tacos. "Where did you get it from?"

"I drove out to a small town where they farm it. It's completely safe. I'll take you out there, if you want."

"So that's where you went the other day? How long is the drive?" She asked.

"It's a couple of hours."

"Yes sir, we will be making a road trip. You're lucky these are good because if it was nasty, you would be bleeding right now. I swear, I don't know where you came from. Who does this?" She grabbed the container and took another bite.

Lexi narrowed her eyes, "I'm gonna finish this burger, and if I die I'm going to kill you." She sighed heavily. "I'm sorry, Bambi."

"I think you have a hit," Hadji smiled.

"I think we do. Now ya'll check out this moonshine that I made."

CHAPTER 16

Buck took a deep breath and called his mom. She had his back on everything, and this would be no different. This time, he had a great idea and was ready to implement it. Shoot, she should be happy that he was trying to make something of himself. He could be his own man and put that school she paid for to good use. He stood in the small bathroom on the trailer and looked in the mirror as he dialed her number. He needed to be confident, sound self-assured. If his mom smelled weakness or any uncertainty on his part, he wasn't going to get a thing. This was a lesson he learned early in life. It's why he could get practically anything he wanted.

His mother answered on the first ring.

"Hey, baby."

"Hey, Ma."

"How are you doing?"

"I'm doing pretty good. Just checking in on you."

"Mhmm. Since when?"

Buck smacked his lips. "Here you go."

"Don't 'here you go' me." She mocked his tone. "I know you love me. I also know you don't call to just check up on me. That's why I'm glad I have your sister. If it wasn't for her I would be all alone without a soul to call on."

Buck shook his head. "You're too much. You're barely in the house, you're not sitting around waiting on my call... but I am gonna do better. I should call you more. My bad."

"What do you want, boy?"

"Why are you trying to rush me off the phone? I can't check up on you?"

"If you must know, I'm out with a friend right now."

"What friend?"

"Boy, mind your business."

Was his mom out on a date? "Who are you with?"

"Buck, what do you want?"

"Is this a good time?"

"You have five minutes to spit it out."

"I have a business idea and I wanted to run it-."

"Wait... before you even finish." She cut him off. "Is this going to require money from me or that I sign a loan, any shenanigans like that?"

"Can I finish first?"

"Can you answer my question?"

"I do need some help, but this is going to be a great idea."

"Just like all your other great ideas, I'm sure. Boy, if you want to build a business, you now own land you can get a pretty penny for. I'm done financing you. You better sell it and bring your butt back here, use that money to open a business. What have you been doing down there anyway? I got the bill for my credit cards, you've lost your mind."

He needed to get her off the subject of those cards quick. "You know New York is expensive. I'm just trying to make it out here."

"Yeah, on my dime. You're too old for this. You've got to stand on your own two feet. Sometimes I think I've spoiled you too much."

He closed his eyes and massaged his temple. Here she went with the same old speech. It was nothing he hadn't already heard before. Whenever he asked her for something, she went into a speech about how she gave him everything. He just had to wait it out and everything would be fine.

After about a half hour, it was glaringly apparent that his mom didn't plan on giving him anything. She wouldn't even let him get the number out of his mouth. She kept talking over him and trying to lecture him further. It was the last thing he needed. What in the hell was her problem? He eventually got her off the phone.

Well, that was a waste of time, he thought to himself. His mom never turned him down. He rubbed a hand down his face and shook his head. It was harder to say no in person, right? He shook his head, flipped the toilet seat closed, and took a seat. Going to see his mom just to get money from her wasn't right. If he went to see her and asked her again, she would cave in, but that felt wrong. It felt like he would be emotionally manipulating her, and he was a man.

It was one thing if she gave in on the first try, but it was another if he begged her. His self-respect would go out the window. She'd already purchased the RV for him. Asking her for another big purchase was too much. Damn, his mom was right. It was time for him to stand on his own two feet and stop begging her for everything. She fronted the bill for the education he didn't finish, she got him every car he ever owned, she stocked his fridge with food, and she'd even gone half-in on his rent with him. Now, he lived off her debit and credit cards. He was a certified mama's boy to the highest level, and this was the first time he'd ever truly felt ashamed. Was he taking advantage of his mom? Or was he simply taking advantage of everything she offered him?

Buck decided that sitting there and feeling sorry for himself wouldn't do him any good. The only thing he could do is move forward. He would have to find another way to come up with the funds for his brand spankin' new dream. It couldn't be that hard to get thousands of dollars and a business plan, surely.

CHAPTER 17

"You know I should kick your butt for what you did, right?" Shante took a sip of her white wine and curled up on the couch with Buck.

He laughed, "I'm surprised you didn't."

"That's only because it tasted so good. I was disgusted and wanted more, at the same time. You can make a whole business off that. You can put it in people's faces what they're eating and they won't believe you. It can almost be like a novelty thing. Tell the truth, and people will want to believe a lie just so that they can have some more. I told myself it was chicken when I ate them. That sauce though, it was so on point."

He pulled her closer to him and kissed the top of her head. "See, that's why I rock with you, you're always giving me good ideas."

Shante giggled, "You could call the burger that Lexi was eating the Bambi burger. It will piss her off and flatter her at the same time. When we left, she couldn't stop talking about it. I still can't believe you got us to come back later and taste that raccoon soup. The spices in that... man, I can still taste it. Only you can make road kill taste like a delicacy."

"It's technically not roadkill because it's farmed."

She smacked her lips, "Whatever, the stuff is roadkill in my opinion. You may as well cook up some cats. If you made them, I would probably eat them. I should remind myself to never bring pets around you. They're not safe."

He shook his head, "I would never do that. You make it sound like I'm some animal murderer. I'm no better or worse than any other meat-eater. As long as it's not people, we're all good."

"See, now you're taking me back to Fried Green Tomatoes. When they served up those ribs and it was really a person's ribs... I don't know why, but that made me laugh so hard when I was little. My mom wouldn't let me watch the movie again. I guess I scared the hell out of her. No one wants to raise a little ax murderer."

"See, I'm the one who should be scared of you, not the other way around. You're trying to barbecue people."

"Whatever, I just thought the irony of the situation was funny. That he was licking his lips and saying just how good the ribs were. It was the best."

"Then you would have loved it when Stan found out what was really in that crock pot," Buck said.

"It's probably good for him that I wasn't there because it's a moment he would never live down. He didn't have any business sticking his spoon where it didn't belong, anyway. Him and Lexi are so cute. I'm kind of salty they didn't want to do a double-date for their first date. It would have been nice to see Lexi tell him what to do all night. You think he's ready for a black girl?" Shante asked.

"What's that supposed to mean? Black girls aren't different from any other girls."

Shante sat up and stared at him. "Really? I know you're trying to be politically correct and stuff, but you don't have to do that with me. I know there's a difference between me and Becky. I don't mind at all, either. I have more attitude than her and a lot more butt."

"You haven't seen white girls lately, huh? They've got those yoga booties now. All plump and stuff."

"Keep it up, Buck. You're gonna have to go get you a Becky."

"With the good hair?"

"You're so stupid. Anywy, what are we going to do about this business? You've gotten all of our hopes up, and we're ready to make some money."

"That's your department."

"What's my department?" She asked.

"The money, of course. I know you didn't think I brought you on board because of your good looks?"

"I was hoping it was the case. I figured I would pass out

a few fliers and get a share of the profit."

Buck looked at her in confusion.

She laughed, "I'm kidding. Let's talk tomorrow night about a game plan because you need capital."

"I'll make sure Stan is there because he's the one in charge of that. He keeps the income coming in and you manage it all."

"I love managing money. I especially love managing a man's money, so this is right up my alley."

"I don't know if I should be scared or turned on."

She kissed him on the lips. "Both."

"See, now I'm gonna have to act on that."

"Oh yeah?"

"What are you going to do?"

"Meet me in the bedroom and I'll show you."

She downed the rest of her wine and ran to the room. Buck was on her heels.

CHAPTER 18

Buck sat in the local bar and took a huge gulp of his draft beer. It was dark and small, just the way he liked it. Fancy bars didn't have the same feel as older ones. Bars weren't meant to be trendy and well-lit, in his opinion. When you were there, it was supposed to be dark and shifty. He loved places where they knew you by name when you entered and kept your favorite drink flowing.

"So how does it feel?" Stan asked.

"It feels good as hell, man." Buck slapped the black folder that sat on the bar.

It was his business license. Buck's restaurant, Wild Food, was officially good to do business. His loan was going to come through any day now, and he had to fight the feeling that maybe he was making a mistake. When he went to get the loan, the loan officer treated him like he was a criminal trying to get over. They checked and rechecked his credentials. Stan went with him and sat open-mouthed as the land was appraised at a hefty sum. Stan whispered to him that maybe he should just sell it and live off it. He could probably sell it at more than it was worth, since it was such a hot piece of property.

Buck couldn't do it. He couldn't sell it. Maybe that made him an idiot, but he'd seen what was happening to the neighborhood. The white people were coming in and buying up all the land and pushing blacks out. Buck couldn't be a part of the problem. His conscious wouldn't allow him to sell out that way. After everything was verified, the bank tried to push to get him to take out more money than he needed, but he stuck with what Stan and Shante suggested. He didn't want to bite off more than he could chew and wanted to ensure he could pay the funds back to keep his property. That's how banks got you. They gave you more than what you need and slapped a ridiculously high interest on it, but he wasn't out here alone. He had backup and excellent advisors.

How did he get so lucky? These people came into his life, and he embraced them without knowing they were all exactly what he needed. He wasn't a man to throw blessings back in God's face. So as long as they all wanted to ride with him, he would appreciate him.

"My mom was so proud." Buck smiled. "I can't lie, I didn't think I could do it. I'm used to her handling everything. It felt good to send her a check for the RV. Everything just seemed so damned hard and I was surprised. There were a bunch of steps, but it was worth it."

Stan nodded. "It says a lot about you. Instead of taking the money and running, you're building something."

"No doubt. I want to have something leave my kids. I don't have any kids yet, I mean, but when I do have them, I want to leave a legacy. I think this food truck will be a good way to learn the business without the huge risk. Once we all get this down, we can move forward with a brick and mortar, maybe opening up a few locations. I know better than to just take the cash and run. My uncle thought enough of me to leave it to me, so I'm going to make him proud."

Stan raised his glass for a toast. "Here's to a new beginning."

"I'm with it." They clinked glasses and took long gulps.

"You know," Stan said, "I'm pretty sure this is going to get me back on the map. No one wants you as an employee until you already have a job."

"I hate that. It's the same with women."

"Not all women," Stan smiled.

"Lexi has you sprung already?"

Stan gave an honest nod. "She's everything I didn't know I wanted. She always has something smart to say. I love it. It's different from the way my ex-wife was. She was mean, but Lexi is playful and witty. I love going back and forth with her."

"So, have you two... you know?" Buck made a lewd gesture with his hands.

"Man, that's none of your business. Do you care to tell me what you and Shante are doing?"

"I got you. I'm glad things are going good between the both of you. I figured it could go either way. Either you two were going to immediately like each other or hate each other. She has that that kind of personality."

Stan nodded, "I can see that. She's so straightforward. I can see how it would rub people the wrong way, but it's a part of her charm. I never have to wonder what she's thinking because she blurts it right out. I like knowing what a woman wants and needs. I'm not a mind reader, and she doesn't expect me to be."

"Dude, are ya'll gonna get married? I think I hear wedding bells?" Buck teased.

Stan almost spit out his drink. "Don't even bring up the M word. I think I'm allergic to that word. I'm enjoying myself, so we'll see where it goes. Oh, I did mean to tell you that I have an interview tomorrow. They emailed me a couple days ago."

"See, I told you things would look up. A white man with a degree will never stay down for long."

Stan shook his head. "It has nothing to do with me being white."

"You really believe that?"

"Yeah, I really believe that. I've worked my butt off to get to where I am. I wasn't handed anything, ever. I come from trailer trash. If I didn't work hard, I would still be there."

"Well, you do still kind of live in a trailer." Buck said.

Stan grinned. "I swear... the more things change, the more they stay the same. I never thought I would voluntarily stay in one ever again. Although, the interior and exterior of the one we have is impeccable. Like I said, it rivals a lot of the places in the area."

"Okay, so I respect your hustle, man. I can't knock you because I wasn't born poor, and look at where I am now. I haven't done bad at all, and I inherited money from family. It's weird because our roles are reversed."

"See, that's the problem. You notice what you said?" Stan said as he motioned the bartender to bring him another drink. "You said our roles are reversed, as if I was supposed to have your life and you were supposed to have mine. That's not true. We get what we get and there's nothing we can do to change that. I'm not entitled to being born in a middle-class family just because I'm white, and you don't have to live in poverty just because you're black."

Buck nodded. "I get what you're saying. You gotta admit, though, if the police were to pull us over, I'm getting arrested and you're getting off with a warning."

Stan sighed heavily. "I would love to be able to argue

with you there, but the world is a messed-up place. It's not right what's happening to black people and how people are turning a blind eye. It's right in our faces, and my people still choose to be blind."

"They see it, they just deny it."

Stan nodded. "I don't even know where to start. My family is totally racist. It's hard to be around them."

Buck laughed. "Have you told Lexi that, yet?"

"I've managed to keep it out of our conversations. If we get to the family meeting, then I will definitely tell her. I'll have to because I wouldn't subject her to my family. They can be a lot to handle. They're angry and bitter. When they find out how successful she is, that will only make them hate her more."

"Good luck, dude."

CHAPTER 19

Buck rubbed his hands together nervously and looked at his friends. "Are ya'll ready for this?"

"Shit, we've come this far, we may as well go through with it. I need to see a return on this investment," Red laughed.

"What investment?" Lexi asked, "Dude, you purchased picnic tables and only because we needed them at the last minute."

Red rolled his eyes, "Whatever, I invested."

"I'm gonna give you your money back," Buck said.

Marlon laughed, "He doesn't want his money back. He wants 20% of the profits."

"That's steep for picnic tables," Stan said.

"Stop wasting time. Opening is supposed to be at 11, and it's 11:01," Shante scolded.

Buck laughed and shook his head. Leave it to Shante to be a stickler for time. She helped him throughout the entire process. She was exactly what he needed. She didn't coddle him, she pushed him to be great. She didn't let him half step on anything. Now, he was about to open his food truck for the first time. He and Hadji were working the kitchen and everyone else was there for support when they were needed.

The idea was so odd and far-fetched, but everyone around him supported him. That was love. He didn't doubt it for a minute.

It was Saturday and the first date of their launch. A huge banner was up, and balloons were all over the place. It felt surreal: the day and time was finally here. He looked around his brand-new, gleaming food truck and admired it. Everything was perfectly in its place. All the meat and food was prepped and ready to go.

This wasn't what Buck saw for himself, as a chef, and his teachers in his culinary program would lose their minds if they saw what he was doing. Granted, some of them may have been impressed. Using proteins that aren't typical is a skill; they're difficult to cook because most haven't perfected it. Southern cuisine has often been dismissed as poor people's food, but Buck always found it to be flavorful and satisfying. Now that he'd added Hadji's spices to his dishes, his food was a Soul food and Indian fusion.

"Umm hello! Open the truck, doofus," Shante laughed.

"Oh, my bad. Should we pray first?" Buck asked.

Shante rolled her eyes and sighed, "How can I say no to

that? Let's make it quick and get this going."

Shortly after, Buck rolled the metal door up and was pleasantly surprised to see a line of people waiting.

Shante beamed, "This is why I wanted you to open up. The people are waiting."

"They sure are." Lexi said as she and Stan stood amongst the crowd. "I've been spreading the word that this is the place to be, so let's start getting these people some food!"

The crowd began to clap. It had to be at least a crowd of 50 people; Buck was in awe.

"You going to stand there looking crazy, or are you going to get to servin' people?" Red asked. "I don't have all day to see this. I've gotta get to cutting hair in an hour."

"How about you just get out of my kitchen? So that the masters can work?"

"Well damn, let me get out of your way, then." Red and Shante exited the truck, leaving Hadji and Buck aboard.

Buck looked at the man who quickly was becoming his best friend. "You ready to do this?"

Hadji nodded, "Let's do it."

Buck looked at the woman who stood in line and gave her his best smile, "How are you doing today, ma'am?"

"Hungry," she grinned.

"I think I can help with that. What would you like?"

"I want an order of the wild turkey sliders and a sweet tea."

"Coming right up." Buck took her card from her hand and processed her payment as he told Hadji the order.

The woman stood to the side as Buck took the next person's order. "What will you be having today?"

The man looked at the menu on the front of the truck and tapped his foot. "Hmm, I'm not sure. I'm stuck between the Bambi burger and tree jumper tacos. What do you like best?"

"I think you'll love the Bambi burger," Buck said.

"Oh, yeah?"

"Yeah, it's seasoned just right." Buck said convincingly.

"Cool, I'll go with that."

Buck told Hadji the order and processed the payment. The man would have liked either order, Buck was sure of it, but the Bambi burger was more money.

After about an hour, many customers had their food. Some took it and walked away, while others stood around on the lot and talked to friends.

One of the guys Buck met when he first arrived stood in front of the line and laughed. "Hell nah. I can't believe you got a damned food truck out here. I can't knock yo hustle, that's for damned sure. So tell me, what kind of meat are you using for this food anyway, because this is wild. I'm reading these names and I'm buggin' the hell out."

Buck shrugged, "It's healthy and good for you. The Chinaman will tell you something is chicken when you know it isn't, and you'll eat it anyway. Pretend this is chicken and enjoy."

The man frowned, "Am I gonna get sick?"

Buck laughed, "Nope."

"You can't be serious. What's in it, for real?"

"That's a part of the charm," Buck laughed. "It may be chicken and turkey, it may not. It's called a mystery for a reason. I'm not out in the street choppin' up rats, if that's what you're askin'."

"You a cool dude and I'm gone take a risk, but if I find out you skinnin' stray cats, I'm coming for you and I'll blow all of this up."

Buck didn't have any doubt that the man was 100% serious. "Don't worry about it dude, what do you want to order?"

Four hours later, Buck shut the food truck down. They were out of product and back in their trailer.

"It was a hit!" Stan said, clapping his hands together. "Everyone loved it, and the fact you wouldn't give them a straight answer regarding what it was, made it even better. They all had a general idea of what the meat was, but you not saying it directly really got them off. Hilarious."

Hadji shook his head. "People love to be willfully ignorant. They all know what it is, but being able to deny it makes it easier to swallow."

"Literally," Buck laughed.

"So, we have enough product on hand in the trailer to prep for tomorrow, but then we have to make another trip to get more. I had no idea it would be that busy, this fast." Aman said.

"Lexi really did her thing," Stan said. "You should have seen her out there on the street handing out flyers and getting people to come over. She's amazing."

Hadji and Buck looked at each other and laughed.

"Damn," Buck said, "I don't know who is more lovesick, me or you."

"You. Definitely you. You could hardly function today if Shante was out of your site for too long. You should have seen your face when she told you it was time for her to leave."

"That was a rhetorical question. You didn't need to answer," Buck replied.

"Oh, but I wanted to."

CHAPTER 20

Buck awoke the following day full of vigor. The day before wasn't a dream. It was real... his food truck was in the same lot. He was selling food, and in New York. He checked an app on his phone and saw how many likes his pictures got from the day before. His family and friend congratulated him, while other people asked where they could find his food truck.

How crazy was that? Although he'd always had the feeling he would make it big doing something, he never thought it would be this way, and definitely not so soon. Many chefs spent years slaving away in kitchens that weren't their own, but he was running a business that was doing damned good. Sure, it may have been a little premature to say he was successful, but if he didn't believe in himself then who would?

He just needed to focus on recouping the money so he could pay his loan back, plus some, and keep the rest of his profits. With luck, he would have an army of food trucks all around New York. *Nah*, he thought. He didn't need luck, he would make it happen. Things were working out in his favor. Who else could come to New York and make it the way that he had? Only the hungry survived, and he was one of em'.

"You awake?" Stan said a few minutes later at his door.

"Yeah, I'm up."

"Good!" Stan busted through the door and sat on his bed.

"What if I was naked in here?"

"Why would I care? You could cover up and we'd discuss business. So, it looks like some important folks may be coming out soon. We'll want to make sure we stay on top of our game." Stan scrolled through his tablet and pulled up his email.

"Oh yeah, who?"

Stan handed him the tablet. "These are some popular food bloggers who are requesting free samples of your food to talk about."

"Free? I swear, these freeloaders are something else. They need to pay like everybody else. We've got bills to pay."

Stan nodded. "I can see why you would think that, but some of them have huge social media followings and are tastemakers, so I suggest we play nice and give them what they want. It can bring in a lot more people and do us a lot of good in the long run. We could use the free publicity.

All we have to do is give them a free meal. It's worth it."

Buck quickly saw his point. Handing out some free tacos, burgers, and soup wouldn't hurt anybody. If they posted it on their social media account and people saw it, then that could mean a lot of good things for this business. While he didn't like the idea of forking over food to freeloaders, he could see the value in it. "Do they have real jobs, or do they just spend their time eating all day for free?"

"Well, it's not really for free. Some of them have jobs and some of them even charge for their services."

"But they're just bloggers, right? It's not like they're with a major company." Buck scowled.

"Where you're from, it may not make sense to give away food to a person that blogs, but here in New York it's one of the best marketing tools you. If they have a wide audience and they are a big influencer, it may do more for you than getting in a magazine. You get to reach your clients at the grassroot level and you get to have people that they know like and trust telling them that you're worth the trip and money. It doesn't get any better." Stan's eyes lit up as he spoke.

"See, that's what you do what you do, and I do what I do. You just let me know who I'm serving for free and I'll hand over the food. Just make sure it's not too many people."

Stan shook his head. "Stop worrying about the wrong things. Everyone is on their way over here so we can finish prepping for today. Hadji has already taken everything over to the food truck. We're just waiting on you."

"Damn, I thought I was doing something by waking up at seven."

"We've been up since about five thirty. I think we're amped because we see all the possibilities. You're a success story, and this is going to make it big, so make sure you're ready because things are going to go fast."

"That's just the way I like it," Buck shrugged.

"Damn. Poor Shante. How does she deal with you being fast and quick?"

Buck laughed, "Mind your own business and worry about Lexi."

"I don't have to worry about Lexi. She and I are doing really good. She's on her way over here."

"Let me get up because I don't want to hear her mouth."

"Exactly, that's the real reason I came in here, anyway. She said you better be up and ready to work."

"She and Shante think they run me," Buck said.

"Don't they?"

"Yeah."

CHAPTER 21

A month passed since Buck opened the doors to his food truck. So far, things sailed pretty smoothly. He'd made a good name for himself throughout the area, and people made special trips just to see him. He even landed himself a few features in some local media outlets. Although he loved the attention he was receiving, it was getting harder and harder to keep where the meat came from a secret. He hadn't really thought that part out. The only thing he could see was dollar signs and the opportunity to cook what he wanted.

What he was doing wasn't illegal, but it could fall into the unethical category. After all, people had no idea they were eating deer and squirrel. Was it his fault if people asked but didn't truly want to know what they were eating? It was almost like a running joke. They would ask him what was in it, and he would ask them what they thought it was. Buck was pretty sure that most of them knew what they were eating, but they didn't want to acknowledge it because if they did, they would have to pretend they were disgusted and put a stop to the food they'd quickly fallen in love with.

He wondered if they realized who they were talking to. After all, Buck was an unapologetic Southern man who swam in lakes and rivers. He preferred to go outside with no shoes on and to feel the red dirt beneath his feet. Beer and moonshine tasted delicious, and he could hang out in the woods all day. He was so Southern that mosquitoes treated him like family and hardly ever took a bite. People in New York weren't ready for him, and a part of him knew it, but he didn't care. They loved his food and that was all that mattered. So why should he second guess himself and feel guilty?

He drove his newly-acquired meat back to the lot and blasted his music with Shante in the passenger's seat. He hated thinking so much. The truth was that he did feel guilty. He couldn't help but shake the feeling that something catastrophic was going to happen. How long was he going to get away with serving up wild life to New York citizens? Sure, he could switch over to another form of meat before anybody noticed, but then the quality of the food would be compromised and so would his concept. Now, that was something he wasn't going to do. He didn't come to New York to be a regular dude with a basic life.

Buck could see the finish line. According to Shante they were operating in the black and had a great first month. She said that if they can keep it up, he can not only afford to pay back the loan but he could make a killing. He was already thinking of getting more trucks and areas he could put them in. For now, he had to get through the food truck festival. So far, Buck hadn't left the piece of land his truck was parked on. In two days, he would be amongst a crowd of thousands.

"What in the hell is on your mind? Earth to Buck." Shante turned the music down and shifted her body towards him.

Buck frowned, "Hey, that's my song."

Shante waved it off, "That's terrible rap. I don't know how people listen to it. All they do is disrespect women and talk about money. It's annoying."

"So, you're telling me you don't listen to rap? You ain't a Biggie fan?"

"Of course I'm a Biggie fan."

"Biggie wasn't a conscious rapper. He wasn't walking around talking about beautiful Queens and helping the community."

Shante smacked her lips, "Whateva. Biggie is like family. I feel like you're talking about one of my cousins, so watch your mouth."

"What are you gonna do if I don't?"

"Well you know, I tote more guns than roses."

Buck laughed at the Biggie reference and was also impressed. He couldn't be mad at Shante; what he was playing over the radio was trash, but he enjoyed the noise.

A woman who knew real rap was always a gem in his book.

"Don't think you're getting off the hook," Shante said. "What's going on in that big head of yours?"

Buck contemplated making something up and laughing it off, but he didn't want to. Him and Shante had grown closer, and if he couldn't be honest with his lady, then who could he be honest with?

Buck scratched his head and sighed. "Well, I'm just thinking about the business and where I want to go from here. I'm wondering what's gonna happen if, and when, people find out what's in it?"

"Now you choose to worry about this? You wait until we've built the business to have these kinds of reservations? You better buck up, Buck, because we have a business to run. The bottom line is that you're serving delicious food that everyone loves, and none of it is illegal. You get everything from a reputable and legal source. You have nothing to worry about."

Buck nodded in agreement, "I know, but…"

"No but. Once you go down that line of thinking you start attracting bull to yourself, and I know that's not what you want. I hooked up with you on this project because I believed in you, and so did everyone else. We believed in your talent so much that we're investing our time. We don't have a choice but to win. We all have a lot riding on you, so you need to keep it together." Shante reached over and grabbed Buck's hand. "I'm not trying to sound evil or overbearing, I just want you to see you the way we all do. I know we crack jokes and make fun of you but honestly this has been an amazing experience, and we gotta keep the good times rolling."

Buck knew she was right, but he just didn't feel it. Instead of replying, he smiled and nodded.

CHAPTER 22

Buck took a deep breath and wondered where the feeling of anxiety that was overtaking him came from. He was usually cool, calm, and collected. It also felt like an elephant was sitting on his chest, but he was determined to move forward anyway. Nothing was going to keep him from completely killing it at this festival.

"If I call your name one more time and you don't answer, so help me God." A voice yanked him out of his self-induced trance. If he didn't know any better, he would have thought it was his mother. The power and femininity within it sparked a "home" feeling, but there was also something else. His body never reacted to his mom the way that it did with this particular voice.

"What are you gonna do?" Buck asked.

Shante smacked her lips, "Don't test or tempt me." She leaned over and kissed him.

"Ew, I'm gonna need ya'll to chill out with the PDA, especially around all of this food," Lexi said. Her voice was teasing as she laid her head on Stan's shoulder.

Before Buck could answer, there was a loud knock on the door of the food truck.

"Ya'll gonna open up or do we have to blow this truck up?" Red yelled.

Hadji chuckled and shook his head, "Is he always this violent?"

Shante rolled her eyes, "He doesn't know anything but violence. He's always talking about how he's gonna cut somebody. As long as he hasn't pulled a switch blade on you, consider yourself lucky. You may wanna open that door before he embarrasses us in front of all these white people." She laughed, "No shade to you, Stan."

Lexi laughed, "He'll be alright. After meeting his family a couple days ago, he needs to catch all of this shade."

"Oh?" Buck looked at Stan. "Dude, I didn't know you took her to see your family. You didn't waste any time, did you?"

Stan smiled sheepishly, "I couldn't help it. It was on my mind, and I figured it would be a good idea."

"Let me just say, his family makes my ghetto family look like the Tanners." Lexi shook her head.

"The Tanners?" Hadji asked.

"Please tell me you've seen Full House?" Lexi said.

Shante laughed, "Lexi, you're so corny. Black people didn't watch Full House. Now the Cosby show, on the other hand…"

"You lie! I watched it. Old episodes would come on TV, and I loved that show." Lexi cut her eyes at Shante.

"I wasn't playin'! I will cut every one of ya'll in there. We can hear you talking. Are ya'll really gone make us stand out here like we can't hear you." Red yelled.

"I'm not opening that door now," Hadji stepped away from the door.

"He's not gonna cut me. He doesn't want these problems," Shante said as she pushed passed everyone in the food truck. "Those of us that aren't cooking need to get the hell out of here, anyway. Buck and Hadji have a lot of work to do, and I gotta keep them on their toes. Everyone else needs to be out there getting people to bring their butts in here."

She opened the door quickly, "Marlon, please tell your ghetto boyfriend to keep his mouth shut before we get put out of the festival. You know it doesn't take much for them to put black folks off of stuff. He may be white, but the rest of us are not."

Marlon laughed, "I can't tell him anything. He doesn't listen to me. I've been trying to teach him patience for a long time now."

"Why are you doing such a poor job?" Shante asked.

"I ran out of patience," he shrugged.

"Okay, ya'll two can stop talking about me like I'm not out here. Are we gonna get started so we can make some money, or what? It's hot out here." Red crossed his arms and tapped his foot like an impatient child.

Buck looked at his watch. "Okay, we have about an hour and half before they open the doors. We need to finish prepping and get this ball rolling. Red is right. We've spent enough time standing around and talking." He took a deep breath and steadied himself.

This was the first time he felt a part of something bigger than himself. It was one thing to run a business on his own lot and allow people to come to him. It was another to put himself in the position to be compared to at least a hundred other businesses. It was now or never. He could hear his mom's voice in his head tellin' him it was a sink or swim scenario. One thing was for certain: he had no intentions of sinking. He spent a nice chunk of change to get his spot amongst the other food trucks and had a lot riding on it. It could be the first step in getting another food truck. It was already on his mind. If people from other areas in New York began to rant and rave about his food on social media, he would have it made. The reviews were already good but he needed more and it was right at his fingertips, he could feel it.

Two hours later, things were going okay. They had a slow but steady stream of clients coming to the truck. Buck looked out the window to the truck next to his; it was a cupcake truck, pink and gold. The line was ridiculous.

Compared to his own, he looked like a scrub.

"No, what you're not going to do is get depressed over this," Shante said. "It's not a big deal and things have just started. People need to warm up to the cuisine you're offering and trust me, they will."

Buck nodded. "You're right. I need to not let this get to me. I can't get anywhere by thinking the worst. The crew is out there doing their thing, so I'm just gonna trust em."

"That's all you can do," Hadji replied. "Remember, a lot of these trucks are already famous, and people came just for them. Next year, trust me, that will be us, but we have to ride out the beginning stage."

Buck knew he was right. He needed to get his head in the game. Feeling sorry for himself wasn't going to help anything. It wasn't like he didn't have any customers, and the day had just started. It was just that he expected more people. He expected to be slammed with so many orders it was tough to keep up. But the pace was surprisingly manageable.

"You gonna take some more orders, or do you need me to do it?" Hadji asked.

Buck snapped out of the daze he was in. "I'm sorry. I didn't realize I was zoning out. I'm buggin'. I'm gonna do it."

Buck turned around and smiled at a black woman who reminded him of his mom. She looked to be in her late to mid-50's. He smiled brightly, "How can I help you?"

"I want an order of your jumper tacos and a small cup of your black eye soup. It's hot as hell out here, but it sounds really good."

"It is really good," Buck confirmed. "No complaints yet."

Buck told the order to Hadji and took the next few orders. This was what life was all about, for him. Serving up great food, making money, and talking to people. It was a dream he thought he could never have, and here it was, staring at him in the face.

He envisioned opening a restaurant, and his mom told him he could have it if he wanted it, but what kind of business was he supposed to have in Lumpkin, Georgia? Now Buck realized why he felt so lazy all the time and why he never wanted to do anything with his life. It was because he wanted more, but he couldn't see it for himself. The life he wanted felt out of his reach. It was here now. It was right in front of his face. Success smelled like spices and savory meat. It smelled like squirrel, turkey, and deer. The words Hadji just told him began to run through his head.

He needed to listen to him. Isn't that what other cultures did? Start from the bottom doing stuff that most people wouldn't so that they could live the lives that others could only dream of? Now he had business partners, a girlfriend, and a life in New York. His resolved strengthened, and he was determined to make his business work by any means necessary. No one was going to stand in his way. Especially not himself.

"Whoa, is this real squirrel?" The woman who reminded him of his mother asked.

Buck winked at her, "What makes you think that?"

"Boy, I'm not stupid. I'm from the South and I know what squirrel tastes like. I thought this was just a novelty name but you're out here serving real squirrel? You're bold." She laughed before took another bite out of her taco.

"Wait, what?" a man in the line asked. "It's actually squirrel? You're chopping up squirrels off the street and giving them to us?"

Buck did his best to keep his composure and to remain calm. He knew this moment would come sooner or later.

CHAPTER 23

Just as quickly as his career began, it was about to end. Suddenly, he felt grateful that there wasn't a massive crowd of people surrounding him. How long did he think he could get away with it? He and his friends were insane to think they could go on forever without disclosing where the meat came from. He was surprised he got away with it for this long. Lying about it didn't make any sense because that would only prolong the inevitable. Buck saw his future going up in smoke. He would have to sell the truck and possibly the plot of land he remained parked on because they would crucify him if he stayed. Once they found out they were eating squirrel and raccoon, it was over.

He just wanted to make food that people loved. Why did the kind of meat matter, as long as it was safe and delicious? That's what he missed about the South. They weren't pretentious over the cut of meat, just the flavor. In New York, the same people who would eat raw fish and squid, thought chitterlings were disgusting. He found that absurd. How can you eat an uncooked animal with soy sauce on it but then judge a cooked intestine? He'd seen the videos on social media. Sometimes there were living organisms still on or in that fish.

He saw his friends and Shante starting to make their way back toward him. Buck thought quick because he didn't want it to be something they all had to deal with. Although they helped him tremendously, it was his business and his burden to carry. They shouldn't have to deal with the embarrassment of everyone finding out the truth.

Hadji cleared his throat behind him and stepped forward but Buck shook his head. "No, I've got this, but thank you."

"You sure?" He asked.

Buck nodded solemnly. It felt like the death of his business.

"Well, you all," Buck smiled. "I'm a Southern man, so my cuisine is authentic and Southern. That means I'm serving squirrel, deer, raccoon, and more. I've given clear indications of what the food is, I haven't tried to hide it. That's why I have the name Bambi burger and so on. It's always been my dream to bring my love for deep Southern food out to New York."

"Awww, hell naw," one black man said loudly, "Buddy out here chasing squirrels and serving them up to us."

"No," Buck said quickly, "I buy all of my meat from

reputable places that follow strict guidelines. These aren't wild animals. They are bred and farmed just like the cows and chickens you eat."

The women who reminded him of his mom gave him a knowing smile, "I knew it. I have to get my son and bring him over here. I've been telling him about this kind of food, but he swears it won't taste good. This is delicious."

"I don't care how delicious it is. I'm not eating raccoon," a white girl said.

Everyone broke out into chatter and some people who'd gotten their food looked at it suspiciously. Some people backed away and walked off without saying anything. Others stood there out of pity before they broke eye contact and walked away.

Shante approached with a worried look. "What in the hell happened? Is everything okay?"

Buck shook his head, "Nah, it's not okay. I messed up big time. I don't know what I was thinking, trying to do this business."

Marlon approached, "What are you over here whining about?" Buck didn't know what to say. He already felt down about what happened. It was over. People found out what he served and they were gone. They were probably gonna tell everyone, folks would freak out, and he would have to hide his face for a while. Man, that shit sucked. He didn't even want to look at what was going to happen to his business on social media. People speculated but now that he verified, it was over.

"I told them," Buck said.

"Told them what?" Marlon asked.

"I told them the ingredients," Buck said.

"Okay, it's legal...so what's the issue?" Red asked.

"The issue is that people don't really want to eat raccoon, they just want to think that they're eating it. It's weird as hell. Kind of how people know that McDonald's chicken nuggets are made of connective tissue and crushed up beaks and how people know that hot dogs are made out of some pretty disgusting parts of the pig, but they eat it anyway. People like to be tricked, they like the illusion of eating something that's familiar, even when they know that it's not what they thought, but they don't want to stop because it tastes good." Buck stopped talking when he saw how his friends were looking at him. It was with a mixture of shock and pity. They looked like they felt sorry for him, and that only made him feel worse.

He didn't need or want their pity. In fact, he didn't deserve it. They all put their time and energy into him and his business, and he failed them.

"We can figure this out," Shante insisted. "It doesn't have to end here. These people don't determine whether you're going to sink or swim. This is one experience. More people will come this way."

"You don't think word is going to get out? They're going to tell everyone, and no one is going to want to come here. We're done. I think we're delaying the inevitable."

"Yeah, you're whining," Marlon rolled his eyes. "Dude, I'm a gay barber. Most men claim they don't want to sit in my chair. I've been cursed out, ridiculed, and even spit on. Do you think that stopped me? I cut hair because I love it, and no one is going to stop me. Now, I have a long list of regular customers. If I quit, then I never would have given myself the opportunity to succeed. Stop it with this defeatist attitude and let's think of a way to push this product."

"You make it sound like we're selling drugs," Buck said.

"It may as well be a drug because your goal is to get people hooked and coming back. You better learn how to adapt, and fast, because we didn't put this much time into this business for it to flop. Do you understand?" Marlon said.

Buck took a deep breath and tried to pretend he wasn't completely freaked out. What was he supposed to do? Should he pack up his truck and leave? What if more angry people came and embarrassed him?

"Okay," Buck said. "Let's leave today and come up with some strategies. We have to be up front, and I'm sure there's going to be a ton of clean up and sucking up I have to do in order to make it right."

"The last thing you should do is suck up," Shante said. "If they smell blood in the water they're going to attack you like a bunch of hungry sharks. You can't be weak. You never said this stuff was chicken, so people ate it at their own risk. That was a part of the allure, and it's not your fault they chose to live in ignorance."

All of that sounded good to him, but he knew how people were. They would attack you no matter what. Maybe if he gave back the remaining money to the bank, sold the truck, and worked his butt off, he could get back to ground zero without taking a huge hit. Moving back home wasn't an option; now he was too addicted to the life in New York. Selling his land would get him a pretty sizable amount of money. That would give him some time to sell his RV, get a small car, and find a place. He wouldn't be poor, but he would need to start a new business venture or find a new source of income, because being a bum wasn't an option.

"Okay," Buck finally said. "Let's get ready to go and then do a game plan. Right now, I just want to get the hell out of here. I've been embarrassed enough for one day."

All of Buck's friends looked at one another as if trying to decide if they were going to honor his wishes or not. After a few seconds, Stan said, "Okay, let's get this show on the road. I doubt if we can just drive out, but we can shut things down and come back later. I'll grab one of the contacts here and let them know we have to leave because of an unavoidable emergency and we'll be back for the truck this evening."

Buck nodded, knowing it was the end of the road for him. There was no need to discuss it with them yet because it was tense enough, but he could tell them everything was done.

Shante entered the truck and closed the window. She looked at Buck with soft eyes, "Are you sure?"

"I'm sure," he said.

"Okay, then we will get out of here," she said.

A loud banging startled them. "Ya'll may want to open this," they heard Lexi scream through the metal shutter. Buck raised it and saw three women standing there with a look of amusement on their faces. Buck was confused. "Can I help you?"

"You're here to serve food, right? We want some," one of the women said.

"Yeah, is it true you serve squirrel? I wanna taste it!" A girl who looked no older than 20 chimed in. "I heard the Tree Jumper Tacos were bomb. I gotta try it, where else can you get squirrel that's safe to eat? It's not like I can just pick one up off the street."

All of them nodded in agreement before the third woman said, "I want to try that raccoon soup. I haven't had raccoon since I was a kid. My great grandma used to bring it back from down south, cook it up, and make burgers with it. So good."

Lexi stood behind them with a big smirk on her face. "Don't just stand there looking dumb. Give the ladies what they want."

Buck was in awe. Behind them Buck saw a man pointing to his food truck and yelling to a group of people, "This is the Truck they were talking about right here. This is the one that makes the authentic Southern cuisine."

Buck blinked rapidly. Authentic Southern cuisine? Is that what people were saying now?

Shoot, it sounded good to him, and he wasn't going to fight it.

EPILOGUE

1 Year Later...

Business deals were made in New York every day, but this one was special. Buck sat at the table with Stan to his left and Shante to his right. On the other end of the table was the old owner of the restaurant and his lawyer. After the paper work was signed, Buck was in a state of mild shock because his dream had just come true, to own a Brick and Mortar restaurant. The location was in a high traffic middle-class area, and he couldn't have asked for more. He managed to make "wild food" a pleasurable dining experience.

He looked around the mid-sized restaurant and already saw the changes he wanted to make. One wall would be exposed brick, and sconces would line the restaurant. People could soon come and get their wild jumper tacos with a glass of bourbon or moonshine.

"Wow," Shante said, breaking the silence. "We've gone

from three food trucks to finally having a restaurant." She laughed. "It only took a year. This is amazingly insane." She grabbed Buck's hand as her engagement ring glistened in the bright light of the restaurant.

Buck nodded and brought his fiance's hands to his lips. "You're absolutely right."

Stan smiled brightly, "I'm officially a Chief Operational Officer. I mean, I was before, but now that we have an actual restaurant, wow."

The old owner and his lawyer stood to their feet.

"Congratulations," the owner said with a big smile. "It's been a pleasure to have this place, but my wife is ready to retire and move to an island, and I'm going to give it to her. I'm about 10 years too late, I'm surprised she stuck with me this long. Now, it looks like you have a journey of your own." He smiled at Buck and Shante. "Ownership of a restaurant isn't easy, I'm sure you already know that from your food trucks, but it's satisfying. Don't be afraid of change, and don't allow your stubbornness to keep you from making money. I've seen a lot of places come and go because of their unwillingness to adapt. It's a shame."

Buck stood up. "Thank you for the advice. I will definitely take it."

An hour later, Buck posted the outside of the restaurant on Instagram telling everyone what was coming in a few months. The responses were almost instantaneous and were positive. Everyone couldn't wait to visit their location.

Lexi, Marlon, Hadji, and Red joined them as they all sat in the empty restaurant, drinking to congratulate themselves on their success.

Buck stared at Lexi and Stan with a little envy because the two married loved birds couldn't get enough of each other. They went and eloped six months before and were still in the honeymoon phase of their marriage. Buck had a feeling their honeymoon period was going to last a long time because they didn't show any signs of slowing down soon. Buck would marry Shante in a heartbeat, but she wanted a huge wedding, and those took time. It would only be seven more months until she was officially his wife.

Hadji, on the other hand, only had another couple of weeks before his wife came to the states to live with him. He was finally able to afford her immigration and couldn't wait for the day he got to hold her in his arms again.

Red and Marlon were the same. They still went back and forth over whether they wanted to get married or not. Red wanted to do it and Marlon swore it was a pointless piece of paper. The jury was still out on if they would do it, but whatever they decided, it was a lifetime partnership.

Everyone now had their own place, and the RV was back home with Buck's mom. She wanted to give him the money for it, but he refused. She now used it to travel and even came to see Buck a couple of times. Buck couldn't bring himself to sell the plot of land his uncle left him. Building on it didn't seem like the right thing to do, either, as the area didn't need another apartment building. What else was there for Buck to do? He chose to build a community garden. It was great for the neighborhood and a non-profit that gave back to the community.

Things were going better than Buck could possibly imagine. He had everything he wanted and was surrounded by people that loved and cared for him. He couldn't wait to see what the future had in store and knew, whatever it was, it was going to be interesting.

ABOUT THE AUTHOR

Homer McMillian is a husband and father of six. It was his desire to follow his late sister's dream to write a book that everyone could read. He feels there is more to urban books than drugs and violence. It's his hope to inspire and encourage aspiring black authors to write books that are humorous and to give the world a little more comedic relief.

Homer is a Bronx native and a former New York City bus driver. He currently lives in Bridgeport Connecticut with his family. You can find him spending most of his days with his younger daughters and raising chicken and ducks.

Contact the Author

Homer would love to hear from you. You can contact him via email or stay in touch via his website.
Site: www.BuckFoolz.com
Email: buckfoolzthebook@gmail.com

Made in the USA
Middletown, DE
26 January 2020